273

Coming closer, he could see that Jonas was half out of the window with excitement . . . But she should never have got into the car at all. She knew the rules . . . Then he was level with the car and peering at the figure behind the wheel.

'Hello, Sean,' said his father.

At first, Sean doesn't see anything wrong with going for a burger with his father, even if it's not his regular day for visiting. But when the meal stretches to a weekend on a boat, and they end up in France, Sean begins to wonder if his father is telling him the truth. Why won't he let Sean phone his mother? And who is Isabella, the Spanish girl his father has brought with him? Sean starts to wonder if he and his sister, Josie, will ever see their mother and their friends again.

Harriet Graham was born in London of theatrical parents and evacuated to Devon during the Second World War. After leaving school she spent a year teaching in India before briefly becoming an actress. After her marriage and the birth of her two sons, she began writing short stories for radio, and her first children's book was published in 1971. In 1985 she became a Tourist Guide and now spends the summers working as a guide and the winters writing. She lives in Portugal and has six grandchildren who keep her in touch with the currency of childhood.

# A Far Away Place

# A Far Away Place

### Harriet Graham

**OXFORD**
UNIVERSITY PRESS

# OXFORD

## UNIVERSITY PRESS

Great Clarendon Street, Oxford OX2 6DP

Oxford University Press is a department of the University of Oxford.
It furthers the University's objective of excellence in research, scholarship,
and education by publishing worldwide in

Oxford New York

Athens Auckland Bangkok Bogotá Buenos Aires Cape Town
Chennai Dar es Salaam Delhi Florence Hong Kong Istanbul Karachi
Kolkata Kuala Lumpur Madrid Melbourne Mexico City Mumbai Nairobi
Paris São Paulo Shanghai Singapore Taipei Tokyo Toronto Warsaw

and associated companies in Berlin Ibadan

Oxford is a registered trade mark of Oxford University Press
in the UK and in certain other countries

British Library Cataloguing in Publication Data available

ISBN 0 19 275147 6

1 3 5 7 9 10 8 6 4 2

Typeset by AFS Image Setters Ltd, Glasgow
Printed in Great Britain by
Cox & Wyman Ltd, Reading, Berkshire

Polly's book

# 1

To begin with everything happened very fast. The waiting and the watching were to come much later. It was then, during the long, hot afternoons when nothing but the cries of the circling birds far above their heads broke the silence, that Sean would go over and over it all in his mind, re-running the sequences of that day until they seemed as unreal as an old film. Somehow he ought to have been able to make it different. But how? That was the question he kept asking himself.

It had started as quite an ordinary day, just the usual sort of Thursday. It was October, the week before half-term. That evening, at supper, Sean was going to ask his mum if he could go on the school skiing trip next March. He had a letter about it in his bag. As he headed for the gate with the others at the end of the afternoon he was thinking about the letter, and whether his mum would be able to afford the trip. He started to look for his sister amongst the crowd of first years. Sean was in his final year at Primary. He would be eleven next birthday and moving on to another school. Sometimes he wished that Josie and he were at different schools already. Then he wouldn't have to take her home every afternoon. Some day, he thought, he really would dump her, like he was always threatening to do when she dragged behind and whined about sweets. Then she'd have to find her own way back home. But deep down Sean knew he couldn't bring himself to do that.

'Want to come round to my place?' Tinker asked, catching up with him. Sean shook his head.

'Got to take Josie home,' he muttered. 'As usual . . . '

Tinker nodded. He didn't suggest that Sean could bring Josie along, too. Josie was a drag, Sean thought angrily. It was a wonder he had any friends left.

'Saturday then?' Tinker said. Sean nodded. His mother didn't work on Saturdays. 'After football,' he added over his shoulder. He was still looking for Josie. The other first years were all around him, showing off their paintings and the things they'd made out of egg boxes. Sean frowned.

That was when he heard the horn. Someone was waving from inside the black Ford Mondeo parked further up the street.

'Who are they tooting?' Tinker asked. Sean shrugged. He didn't know anyone with a black Ford. There was another blast on the horn.

'I think it's for you.' Tinker frowned.

Sean narrowed his eyes, putting up a hand against the sun. A kid was hanging out of the car window. Then he gave a groan.

'What's up?' Tinker asked. 'Is something wrong?'

'That's Josie in that car,' Sean told him, starting to run.

Coming closer, he could see that she was half out of the window with excitement, waving and calling. But she should never have got into the car at all. She knew the rules. Their mum was always telling them. Then he was level with the car and peering past Josie at the figure behind the wheel. A wave of relief swept over him.

'Hello, Sean,' said his father, and smiled, putting an arm round Josie to stop her bouncing up and down.

'I tooted the horn,' she said, pink and breathless. 'Dad let me—didn't you, Dad?'

'I thought you were coming on Sunday,' Sean said. 'That's what Mum told us—'

'Change of plan,' his father cut in. 'I thought you'd be pleased.'

'Yeah—'course,' Sean nodded.

2

'Well, hop in then. We're going to get a hamburger, isn't that right, sweetheart?'

'Yum yum,' said Josie. 'And a Coke.' She twisted her arm round his neck. 'You promised.'

'And a Coke.' He laughed, his eyes meeting Sean's above Josie's head. For a moment Sean hesitated. Then his father leant across and swung open the car door. 'Let's go,' he said. 'Before that warden up there gives me a ticket.'

Sean looked back over his shoulder. Tinker was still standing near the gate, watching, just in case there was something wrong. Sean gave him a thumbs up and saw Tinker nod in reply. Then he slung his bag on to the back seat and climbed in. The next moment they had pulled away.

'New car,' Sean said, reaching for the seat belt.

'Only picked it up a couple of days ago,' his dad nodded. 'It goes like a rocket on the motorway.'

Sean frowned. A question had formed in his head and kept bobbing about. He'd have to ask. He felt the palms of his hands beginning to sweat.

'Mum knows about this, doesn't she?' he said, leaning forward. 'I mean, she did say it would be all right?'

Ever since their parents split up, Sean's dad got this funny look on his face whenever he or Josie mentioned their mum. But today his dad just grinned at him.

''Course she did,' he answered. 'Stop worrying, old son. Real old worry-guts your brother, isn't he, Josie?'

Josie giggled, twisting herself round inside the seat belt.

'Worry-guts, worry-guts,' she chanted. Sean ignored her.

'Where are we going?' he asked, staring out of the window.

'Hamburgers.' His father's voice was even as he put the car into first gear and roared away from the lights.

'But we passed the High Street ages ago.' Sean frowned.

3

'Thought we'd try a different place today . . . '

'Different?'

'Change of scene. It'll be easier to park.'

Sean didn't know where they were any more. Somewhere in South London, out towards the motorway. For a moment he closed his eyes. Half of him knew that something was wrong. The other half was telling him not to be so daft. They were with their dad, after all. He was taking them for a hamburger. Then they'd go back home and it would be just another boring Thursday.

'I'm thirsty,' Josie had started to whine. 'When will we get there?'

'Soon, sweetheart. Not long now.'

Sean opened his eyes. He could see some yellow signs for a new shopping centre and just beyond them, blue signs for the motorway. They were getting further and further away from home. His palms began to sweat again. He rubbed them up and down on the car seat.

In the restaurant Sean's father told him to wait at the table with Josie while he fetched the burgers and Coke.

'And fries,' Josie called after him.

'And fries,' their dad smiled.

Sean could have run out then. The thought crossed his mind. But he still wasn't sure. And anyway Josie wouldn't budge, he knew that. He shot a quick look through the open door towards the phone kiosk. He'd spotted it on the way in. But he hadn't got any money. He could phone the operator . . . dial 999 . . . Don't be daft, said the other voice inside his head. He's your *dad*.

And then his father was back with the tray of burgers and fries, and behind him there was a woman with another tray; young, tall, with dark eyes and a lot of red-brown hair, shining, twisted into a rope, jeans and a white shirt and a brown leather jacket.

'This is Isabella,' Sean's father said. 'A friend of mine. And guess what—she's coming with us for the weekend. Isabella, this is Sean . . . and Josie . . . say how-do, sweetheart.'

4

Sean leant forward.

'What weekend?' he asked. 'It's only Thursday.' His voice was rising. 'Half-term's next week, you know . . . there's school tomorrow—'

'All right, all right,' his father cut in. 'It's a surprise, I know, but one day off school won't matter—at least, that's what your mum thought.'

'You told her?' Sean said. 'You told Mum?'

'Sure I did,' his father said.

Sean shook his head. 'She never said . . . '

'Rang her first thing this morning at the office. Must have been just after she'd dropped you at school. Stop worrying—and eat that burger before it gets cold.'

Sean watched his father glance across at Isabella who had sat down opposite Josie and was playing peek-a-boo with her over the table. Looking up, Isabella smiled and nodded at Sean's dad, then leant across and picked a bit of fluff off the sleeve of his jacket.

'Tell them about the boat,' she suggested. 'That will be beautiful, eh?'

Her voice was deep and as she moved, waves of her perfume swept across the table.

'A friend of Isabella's has this amazing yacht,' his father was saying. 'That's where we're going—for a trip on it. You always wanted me to take you sailing again, didn't you, old son? We might even go over to France— for the weekend. That would be good, eh?' Sean dabbled one of his fries in the pool of ketchup. He was beginning to feel sick. After a moment his dad turned to Josie. 'You want to go on a boat with your dad, don't you, sweetheart?' But Josie didn't answer either, just shuffled round on her seat kicking the table leg. 'Stop wriggling like that, darling,' her father said.

'Wanna go loo-loo,' Josie said.

' 'Course, darlin'.' He jerked his head at Isabella, who stood up and held out her hand to Josie. Josie hesitated, looking across at Sean.

'Wanna go with Sean,' she said.

'Sean can't go into the Ladies',' said his dad. 'You know that. Go with Isabella, there's a good girl.'

Sean watched them walk upstairs hand in hand. Isabella swung the rope of her red-brown hair back over her shoulder, laughing down at Josie. His mum's hair was short, untidy most of the time, and beginning to be streaked with grey. That was because of her colouring, she said. People with her kind of eyes and skin often went grey early. She ran her fingers through her hair all the time, too, when she was writing, or on the phone, that was what made it so untidy.

'You're very quiet,' his father said. 'And you've hardly eaten a thing. Aren't you hungry?' Sean shook his head. 'You'll like Isabella once you get to know her,' his father went on after a moment, leaning towards Sean. 'A bit sticky to begin with, that's all. But she's been looking forward to meeting you—'

Sean looked up. His heart was beating hard.

'Can I phone Mum?' he asked. 'To let her know we're OK?'

For a second his father's jaw tightened. Then he smiled.

' 'Course you can,' he said.

'Now,' said Sean. 'Can I ring now? There's a phone outside.'

He saw his father hesitate. Then he looked down at his watch.

'She won't be home yet,' he said. 'It's only just gone five. Why not wait till we get to the harbour? There's sure to be a phone there, and you'll be able to talk for longer.'

'OK,' Sean nodded.

Isabella and Josie were coming back down the stairs hand in hand.

'Here they are,' his father said. 'Now hurry up and finish your burgers, you two. We need to get going, or we'll miss the tide. Ship ahoy, eh, lads?' He winked at Sean.

Outside in the car park Sean's dad put an arm round his shoulders.

'You come in front with me this time,' he said. 'Josie and Isabella can go in the back—all girls together.'

'We'll like that, won't we?' Isabella said, swinging Josie by the hand. Josie gave a couple of jumps and nodded, smiling up at Isabella, her eyes as big as saucers. Sean frowned.

On the motorway his father drove fast, pulling out into the overtaking lane, staring straight ahead through his dark glasses towards the setting sun.

West, thought Sean. The sun rises in the east and sets in the west. Out loud he asked: 'Where are we going now?'

'South coast,' his father said. 'The boat's moored on the Solent. We'll be spending the night on the boat. There are plenty of bunks. It's big, Sean. Three times the size of that old sieve we took up the Thames. You'll love it. Honestly!'

Sean closed his eyes to block out the sun, remembering the day they'd spent on the river. His dad had picked the boat up first thing in the morning, hired it for the whole day. His mum had brought a picnic and it had been hot. Trees dipped their branches into the water as they nosed their way upstream, ducks scattered, bobbing away on the ripples their boat made, and people sitting in deckchairs on the bank had waved as they went past. It had been a great day. But that was before everything had gone wrong, before all the rows and the shouting. His mum and dad had been together then.

And then, last year, his dad had walked out. Sean's mum had sat at the kitchen table alone that day, and the tears had run down her face. She'd sat like that for ages. Sean couldn't bear to watch. He went upstairs and played tapes on his Walkman, trying to pretend it wasn't happening, that his dad would soon come back.

But he hadn't. And now it was too late.

The light was fading from the sky when they arrived

at the harbour, but Sean could see the phone kiosk beside the office.

'There it is,' he said. 'Can I ring now? Please, Dad, give me some money—'

'Hang on, Sean,' his father said. 'Don't you want to see the boat first . . . and you could lend a hand with this luggage, too.'

Along the pontoon there were two men waiting for them beside the boat. One of them was called Skip. He seemed to be the boss.

'You're late,' he said to Isabella. 'You told us five o'clock.'

'It wasn't so easy,' Isabella shrugged. 'Anyway, we're here now.'

'And about time, too,' Skip said. 'Is this the luggage?'

Isabella nodded. He jerked his head towards the other man.

'Get that lot down below,' he said, and picking Josie up he swung her across the gangplank and on to the deck. 'You, too, son,' he said, nodding to Sean, and turning to hold out a hand to Isabella.

Sean shook his head. Everything was happening fast. Too fast. He could see Josie's face beginning to crumple into tears. He swung round, meaning to start back towards the telephone box, and saw his father running along the pontoon towards them.

'Hurry, Harvey!' Isabella called. 'We're late . . . ' His father nodded, and before Sean could speak he had caught him by the arm and was half heaving, half pushing him up the gangplank and on to the boat.

'The phone call,' Sean yelled, trying to struggle free. 'You said we could. You promised!'

'Later, Sean. Later, old son. We've got to go now or we'll miss the tide.'

Suddenly Josie was howling, too, catching the panic in Sean's voice. Tears sprouted in her eyes.

'I want Mummy . . . I want to go home . . . I don't

like it here,' she wailed, and wrenching herself free from Isabella she headed for the side of the boat.

'For heck's sake keep that child under control,' Skip shouted.

Already they were pulling away from the pontoon. Looking round Sean could see that the strip of water was too wide to jump. He grabbed hold of Josie's arm.

'I want Mummy, I want Mummy,' she sobbed, trying to fight him off. But Sean held on tight, and bending down he put both arms round her.

'Stop that racket,' he told her roughly. 'It won't do any good—can't you see that?' Josie gulped, wiping her eyes on her sleeve. 'Anyway, I'm here, aren't I?' Sean said before she could begin again. 'I'll look after you.'

Even as he spoke he could feel a kind of weight settling on his shoulders.

9

# 2

'A Ford Mondeo,' Tinker said, pushing his glasses back up his nose. 'Black.'

'Black? But Harvey's car is red,' said Ros Taylor. 'Are you sure, Tinker?'

There were quite a few people in Sean's front room by then. Ros Taylor, Sean's mum, was sitting on the sofa with her brother and sister-in-law. Opposite them in the green easy chair sat the detective constable, and next to him was Tinker's dad. All of them were looking at Tinker.

'Black,' said Tinker. 'Definitely.'

'Go on,' the detective nodded. 'What happened next?'

'Josie was in the car already,' Tinker said slowly. 'That was why Sean went chasing off. He could see her hanging out of the window, you see.' The detective nodded again.

'What happened next?' he asked. Tinker frowned. 'Take your time. No rush.'

It had gone very quiet in the room. Outside, a taxi had stopped somewhere up the street, and Tinker heard a front door bang.

'You remember what happened next, don't you?' the detective went on after a moment. Tinker nodded. He pushed his glasses up his nose and began again.

'When Sean got to the car he bent down and was talking to someone . . . '

'Did you see who it was?' the detective asked. Tinker shook his head.

'I was too far away.'

'And you didn't follow Sean up the street?'

'I was going to,' Tinker said. 'Only after a minute Sean turned round and gave a sign—like this.' He made a thumbs up.

'Like everything was OK,' the detective said, nodding.

'Yeah, that's right. Then he got into the car and they drove off.'

'And you've no idea who was driving the car?'

Tinker hesitated. 'It must have been someone Sean knew,' he said. 'He'd never have got in otherwise. I thought it was probably his dad.'

'But you didn't actually see?' Tinker shook his head.

There was silence for a while. Then Ros Taylor leant forward.

'Can you remember anything else, Tinker? Anything at all? You see, you were the last person to see Sean . . . Sean and Josie.' She broke off.

'Don't worry, Ros,' her brother said, leaning over and taking her hand. 'We'll find them all right. Everything will be OK, you'll see.'

'No,' she said angrily, shaking him off. 'No, everything won't be OK, Bob. I know what's happened . . . I can't prove it, of course—' She looked across at the detective. 'But I know just the same—'

'And what do you think has happened, Mrs Taylor?' the detective asked gently.

'Harvey's taken them abroad,' she said. 'That's what's happened.'

'It's possible,' he nodded. 'But I don't think we ought to jump to conclusions.'

'Not a very big jump, is it?' Ros Taylor said. For a moment no one spoke. She ran her fingers through her hair, staring past them all towards the window. The curtains were still open and the night made a big, black oblong. 'She's such a baby still,' she whispered. 'Oh, Josie . . .'

Tinker hated it when grown-ups cried. He looked

11

desperately round at his dad, as the tears welled up in Ros Taylor's eyes. But it was the detective who came to his rescue.

'I don't think we need keep your son here any longer,' he said. He turned to Tinker. 'You've given us some very useful information, Tinker, but if you do happen to think of anything else, no matter how small, just tell your dad and he can get in touch with us.' He was shepherding them towards the hall as he spoke. Looking back, Tinker could see that Ros Taylor had put both hands over her face and was rocking backwards and forwards.

'Bad business,' Tinker's dad said, shaking his head. 'I hope you find the kids soon.'

'We'll certainly be doing everything we can.' The detective nodded. 'Thanks again, and don't forget, if there's anything else—like the car registration. I don't suppose you can remember that, can you?' Tinker shook his head. 'Pity. That could be important. If you do—give us a bell.'

Outside in the street Tinker was glad of the wind on his face.

'If I'd gone as far as the car with him I'd have known who it was,' he said to his dad.

'Just as well you didn't. We wouldn't want you disappearing, too,' his father answered.

'If it was Sean's dad,' Tinker went on after a moment, 'and if he has taken them abroad—well then, that means—' He broke off, frowning.

'What?' his father asked.

'Nothing,' said Tinker after a moment. He was wondering whether he'd ever see Sean again.

'I daresay it's all a storm in a teacup,' Tinker's father said to his wife that evening after Tinker had gone to bed. 'Harvey's taken the kids off for a long weekend I expect. He'll be back soon enough—Monday morning probably. I can't see him managing that Josie on his own for long.'

12

'I hope you're right, love,' said Tinker's mother. 'But Harvey's a funny chap. Unpredictable, if you know what I mean. Always has been.'

'You're right about that.' Tinker's father frowned.

'I'm glad I'm not in Ros Taylor's shoes tonight,' Pat Johnson said, shaking her head. 'If you ask me she's got every right to be worried.'

Lying in bed Tinker could hear the blurry sound of their voices through the wall, and guessed they were talking about Sean and Josie. He closed his eyes, wondering where Sean was at that moment. Somehow he felt as though he was a long way off. But that's stupid, Tinker thought. You can't tell a thing like that by feeling it.

Being an only child, Tinker had never found it easy to make friends at school. Having to wear specs didn't help. They made him feel like an outsider, different from the others. It was partly because they stopped you doing much sport, and partly because they made you look brainy even if you weren't. Tinker had been lonely until Sean switched classes a year ago and they'd found themselves sitting next to each other. Having Sean as a friend had made all the difference to Tinker. It would be awful at school without him.

If only there was something I could do, Tinker thought, punching his pillow and frowning into the darkness. If I could remember the registration number of the car—the detective said that was important . . . He screwed his eyes tight shut, then opened them, letting his mind go blank. Sometimes he could remember things that way. But nothing happened. Maybe Sean will be back tomorrow after all, he thought, rolling over on to his side. Or Monday . . . He had to come back. He had to—didn't he?

Josie had gone to sleep at last, her face streaked with chocolate, one hand clutching the new pink and blue

13

teddy her dad had given her. Harvey Taylor stood up gingerly, and then bent over to tuck the blanket more closely round her. Josie didn't stir.

'Worn out,' he said softly, closing the cabin door behind him. 'She'll sleep till morning now, I expect.'

Sean was sitting in the angle of the bench seat, hugging his knees. Isabella half turned from the galley where she was cooking eggs and smiled, a lovely lazy smile. Catching the look that passed between her and his dad, Sean laid his cheek against his knees and closed his eyes.

'Hungry?' his father asked. The smell of frying bacon was making Sean's stomach rumble, but he shook his head all the same. 'Why don't we go up on deck and see the stars?' his father said. 'That'll give you an appetite. You'll need your coat—it's cold out there. And here's my scarf.'

'Five minutes, Harvey,' Isabella said. 'You tell the others, please. Ready in five minutes.'

Up on deck the air crackled, frosty and cold against Sean's face making his cheeks and lips feel numb. Seeing him shiver, his father put his arm around him, drawing him close.

'There's the Plough,' he said, pointing towards the stars. 'See? It even looks like a plough, doesn't it? And that one's the Pole Star—the one you steer by when you're at sea.'

Above their heads the white sails spread, smacking gently in the night air, and Sean could hear the hiss of the sea against the sides of the boat.

'Are we really going to France?' he asked, turning to see his father's face.

'I told you,' his father nodded.

'For the weekend?'

'Yep!'

'But what about passports,' Sean frowned. 'Don't we need them—Josie and me?'

He felt his father's arm tighten around him, and when

14

he answered Sean there was a sudden roughness in his voice.

'For Pete's sake stop worrying, old son. Everything's taken care of. I thought you'd enjoy all this—'

'I am enjoying it,' Sean lied. 'It's great . . . but—'

'But what?'

'It's just that I wish . . . I mean, you promised, didn't you? You promised . . . ' His voice tailed away.

'Ah . . . you mean about phoning your mum?' his dad said. 'Yes, she worries too, doesn't she? Just like you. Now listen, old son,' he went on before Sean could interrupt, 'your mum's had you and Josie to herself for over a year now. I think it's my turn for a while, don't you? Fair's fair, after all. I've missed you both,' he went on, his voice gentler now. 'And I just want us all to have a good time together this weekend. Nothing wrong with that, is there?' Sean was silent. 'Or perhaps you just don't want to be with your dad any more?'

'Of course I do.' Sean frowned, shifting uneasily in the circle of his father's arm. It wasn't fair of his dad to talk like that, when all Sean really wanted was for his mum and dad to be together all the time, like they used to be. It wasn't his fault that their dad could only see them at weekends. That's what the Courts had decided. His mum had told him that after the divorce. But Sean couldn't say any of that to his dad, any more than he could say that he wished it was his mum down there now, frying eggs and bacon, instead of Isabella. There wasn't anything he could say.

'Food's ready,' Isabella called through the hatchway.

'We'll talk about this again tomorrow,' Sean's father said. 'And stop worrying. Everything's going to be fine.'

It didn't feel fine though, Sean thought as he dragged the unfamiliar smelling blankets up round his ears and tried to sleep. It felt wrong, as wrong as wrong could be. What were he and Josie doing here on this yacht halfway to France? His dad hadn't said anything about going away for the weekend the last time they'd seen him, or

15

about selling the car. Or about Isabella, come to that. And nor had his mum. He and Josie hadn't even got their toothbrushes with them, and he knew that his mum would never have let them go away for the weekend without any clean clothes or washing things. It all added up to just one thing. His mum didn't know where they were.

I'll have to phone her tomorrow, he thought, feeling the sway of the yacht as it carved onwards through the water. Somehow I'll have to find a way.

# 3

When Sean woke up Josie was standing beside him in her vest and knickers, and shaking him by the shoulder.

'Where am I?' she demanded. 'Sean! Wake up—wake up now!' Sean gave a groan, and tried to huddle back under the bedclothes.

'Go back to bed,' he muttered. 'It's too early. Can't you see? It's not even properly light yet.'

'Tell me,' Josie persisted, tugging at his blanket.

'Oh, go away,' Sean told her crossly.

'Only when you tell me.'

'We're on a boat,' Sean said, seeing that she wasn't going to give up. 'You remember . . . with Dad. There. Now go back to bed . . . please, Josie.'

She stared at him and slowly shook her head.

'Don't want to,' she said, still holding tight to the blanket. 'Where's Mum? I want Mum . . . '

'Mum's not here,' he said. 'She's at home. And we're with Dad. For the weekend. I told you.'

'Isabella's here, isn't she?' Josie asked after a moment. Sean nodded. 'I don't like this boat anyway,' she said. 'I want to go home. Why can't we go home?'

Sean frowned. 'Because . . . because we're going to France,' he told her. 'In fact,' he went on, suddenly realizing that the yacht wasn't moving, 'I think we might be there already.'

Wriggling out from under the blankets he knelt up on the bunk and looked through the porthole. A strip of pearl grey water divided them from the land. Beyond it

17

Sean could see a line of buildings, and he knew at once that they were no longer in England. Even the church tower rising above the roofs of the town looked different from an English church tower. Sometime during the night, while he and Josie had been asleep, they must have reached the French coast. And as soon as it was light Sean guessed that they would sail into the harbour.

'Let me see.' Josie had scrambled up on the bunk and was kneeling beside him. She pushed her nose against the glass. 'Is that France?'

'It must be,' Sean nodded. Suddenly he grinned, thinking how surprised Tinker would be when he told him on Monday that he'd been to France for the weekend on a yacht. There was a faint, pink tinge in the sky now, as though the sun would soon rise. A couple of fishing boats chugged slowly towards the harbour, their wash rocking the yacht a little so that Sean had to put up a hand to steady himself. A few days, his dad had said. He just wanted to have them to himself for a few days. Well, a weekend was a few days. When the weekend was over, they'd go home. Everything was going to be all right after all, Sean thought, watching Josie blow on the glass and then draw a circle and some splodgy dots with her finger.

'What's that meant to be?' he asked.

'A cat, of course,' she said, putting in another splodge.

'Looks more like a chocolate chip cookie to me,' Sean said. She gave him a cold look and started on another circle with splodges.

Sean sat down on the bunk again and pulled the blankets up round his shoulders. He could see the cabin quite clearly, now that it was getting light, but there was no sound from the second cabin, so Sean guessed his dad must still be asleep. Remembering the comic in his school bag, he slithered out of bed.

Down at the end of the cabin, where it narrowed to a point, a chunk of it had been sectioned off to make a couple of lockers. Sean had seen his dad putting some things in there the night before. That was where his school bag would be.

In the first locker there was nothing but a pile of life jackets. He opened the second locker. Inside were all the plastic carrier bags from the boot of the car, and sticking out from underneath them at the very bottom of the pile, Sean could see the strap of his school bag. But as soon as he started to pull, everything came out at once.

Bored by her circles and splodges, Josie clambered off the bunk and squatted down beside him.

'What's in there?' she asked, reaching for one of the plastic bags.

'How should I know?' Sean said. 'Leave it alone, Josie. Those bags are Isabella's.' He began to look for his comic. By the time he'd found it, Josie had emptied the first two plastic bags on to the ground and was sitting amongst a pile of clothes. Sean stared in astonishment. They certainly weren't Isabella's clothes.

'Look,' Josie purred. 'This is for me. See! A new T-shirt . . . and pink shorts—look, Sean.' He let the comic drop and knelt down beside her, frowning. 'And these are for you,' Josie went on, diving into the heap of clothes and pulling out jeans and a couple of checked shirts. Everything was there. Underpants, knickers for Josie, socks, even two dressing gowns. Sean's palms had begun to sweat as he stared at the pile of clothes. They were all brand new. They still had their labels on them.

Josie was tugging a pale blue T-shirt over her head.

'Stop it,' Sean shouted suddenly. 'Stop it, Josie. Put those things back.'

'But it fits me,' she said. 'Look! Anyway, I like it.'

'It doesn't belong to you,' he told her, his voice rising. 'None of these things do. Take it off.'

But Josie only shook her head. Then she grabbed the pink shorts before Sean could put them back in the bag, and began capering round the cabin and flapping them at him.

'No!' Sean yelled, stretching out his arm to catch her.

'Give them to me, Josie.' She giggled, climbing on to the bunk. Sean grabbed her and tried to wrench the shorts out of her hands, but Josie gave a shriek and kicked out at him. Neither of them heard the cabin door open.

'Hey, hey, you two . . . what's going on? Why the racket!'

Sean felt himself being lifted up and dumped at the other end of the bunk. Then he heard his dad say, 'Ah-ha! I see you found the clothes then.'

He opened his mouth to explain, but Josie got in first. 'It was Sean's fault,' she wailed. 'He said the pink shorts weren't for me . . . and they are, aren't they? Because they fit . . . and now he's hurt my arm.' She gave a gulp. 'Look, Daddy!' He sat on the bunk and lifted Josie on to his knee.

'Of course the shorts are for you,' he said. 'And the T-shirt . . . and lots of the other things. And Sean didn't mean to hurt you, I'm sure . . . did you, Sean?'

Sean was staring at the pile of new clothes on the floor. He'd just realized something. They were all summer clothes. And it was October—the beginning of winter.

'Did you?' his father said again.

'Did I what?' Sean frowned.

'You didn't mean to hurt Josie's arm, did you?' Sean shook his head. 'Well, say sorry then.'

'Sorry,' he muttered.

'There. Now Sean's said he's sorry . . . so stop crying, there's a good girl, and let's have a look.' Josie's sobs petered out and she turned a sideways look on Sean. 'Isabella chose these shorts for you,' their dad went on. 'Let's see if they fit.'

A moment later Josie was pulling the pink shorts on, all smiles.

'There are some things for you, too,' his father said, standing up and reaching into the pile on the floor. 'This stripy T-shirt, and the blue shorts.' Sean shook his head. He hated trying on clothes at the best of times. If he didn't try them on everything might still be all right.

'Go on,' his father said. 'Just the shorts, then.'

'Do I have to?' Sean asked. 'Anyway, what's the point? These are all summer things.'

His father looked at him. Then he smiled. After a moment he said, 'Well, what about the dressing gown then?' Sean shook his head.

'I've got a dressing gown at home,' he said. 'I don't want another one.' It sounded rude, but he didn't care.

'Isabella will be disappointed,' his father said. 'She chose everything herself.'

Sean shrugged. He didn't care about Isabella either. He turned away and stared out of the porthole. If he was at home he'd probably be halfway to school by now, he thought. He and his mum and Josie. She always walked with them as far as the school gate. Then she went off to catch the bus to her office. He knew his dad was looking at him, but he just kept staring out at the roofs of the town. It was History first thing this morning. History, Maths, Break. Then PE. Friday was the best day of the week. Only he wasn't there. Something was wrong. Sean knew it for certain now, ever since he'd seen the summer clothes. And he didn't know what to do.

Isabella put her head round the door.

'Breakfast,' she said.

'Look, look, see my shorts,' Josie crowed, dancing round the cabin. 'Sean's naughty—he won't try his new things on. Dad asked him, but he won't . . . will you, Sean?'

'That'll do, Josie,' his dad said, reaching out an arm. But Josie wriggled past him and ran to Isabella.

'It's true,' she said. 'He won't even try the dressing gown. He doesn't like his things.' She slewed round to look at Sean. Isabella was looking at him, too. Then she smiled.

'Later,' she said, stroking Josie's hair. 'Sean will try his clothes later. Come now, let's have breakfast. Sean—

21

you get dressed, too. Then you can both choose your cereal. It's Variety Pack.'

They were halfway through their cereal when Sean heard the engine start up. His mind began to race again. They'd be leaving the yacht soon. Already he could hear rustling from the cabin as Isabella stuffed everything back into the plastic bags. He must do something quickly, before it was too late. Somehow he must find a way to phone home. There would be a phone box on the harbour, he thought. He glanced at Josie. She was humming to herself, scooping milk and sugar out of her bowl. He leant forward and took hold of her wrist, but gently. She looked up.

'We're going to be in France soon,' he said quietly, shuffling closer to her along the bench. 'Perhaps Dad will let us phone home. You'd like to talk to Mum, wouldn't you?' Josie nodded. She was holding her breath, looking at him. Sean glanced towards the cabin. 'I know we can't see Mum—' he went on.

'Why can't we see her?' Josie asked.

'Because we're in France and she's in England,' Sean said. 'But we could talk to her—on the phone—tell her we're all right . . . you know.' Josie nodded, her brown eyes solemn. Inside the cabin Isabella was starting to put all the carrier bags in a pile. 'Why don't you ask Dad if we can phone when we get off the boat,' he went on. 'Will you?' Josie nodded. Sean wasn't sure whether she really understood. 'Because we may not see Mum for a bit,' he went on.

'Why?' Josie asked again. Sean frowned.

'Because she's at home and we're here,' he told her. 'Maybe we won't see her for quite a long time.' Josie opened her mouth to interrupt, but Sean went on quickly. 'If we can't see her, phoning would be the next best thing, wouldn't it? If Dad will let us . . . Only maybe he won't . . . '

'But I want to,' Josie said, her voice beginning to rise. 'I want to phone . . . I want to . . . why can't I?'

Sean heard the sound of footsteps above.

'Ask him then,' he hissed into Josie's ear. 'Ask Dad if we can phone Mum.' He pulled away quickly as his father started down the steps.

'What's up now?' his dad asked. 'Is this you again, Sean?'

Josie had started to wail.

'I want to phone Mum . . . I want to . . . '

Isabella had finished with the bags and was watching from the cabin door. Sean saw his father give her a helpless look and shrug his shoulders as he lifted Josie on to his knee.

'I want Mummy . . . I want . . . ' Her voice was rising again.

'For Pete's sake, Harvey, can't you tell that kid to shut up?' Skip asked, putting his head through the hatchway. 'Mike and I are trying to concentrate up here. Besides, we're coming into harbour, and it doesn't look good, if you know what I mean . . . '

'OK, OK,' Sean's dad answered. He turned back to Josie. 'Stop crying, sweetheart, and tell me what all this is about. You want to phone Mum . . . is that it?' Josie nodded.

'You promised anyway,' Sean said, leaning forward.

'I know,' his dad said. 'Tell you what, dry your eyes and we'll see what we can do.'

'When?' Sean asked.

'Yes . . . when?' Josie asked, screwing her head round to look at him.

'As soon as we get off the boat,' he said. 'There's sure to be a phone on the harbour.'

'You promise?' Sean cut in. His father glanced across at Isabella, who swung the rope of her red-brown hair back over her shoulder with an imperceptible shrug.

'I promise,' his dad said. 'It's early still. We may just catch her before she goes to work.'

She'll be there anyway, Sean thought. Waiting by the phone. But he didn't say anything.

It took a while to get through, what with finding the right money and working out how to dial England, but at last the number was ringing. Sean felt his stomach muscles tighten. Josie had the phone, but his dad was right next to her with one hand on the receiver, helping her to hold it against her ear. After a couple of rings Sean knew his mum had answered by the look on Josie's face, but he couldn't hear what she was saying. For a long moment Josie didn't speak at all. Sean was afraid his mum might hang up.

'We're with Dad,' Josie said at last. 'I've got new shorts and a new T-shirt.' Sean started to fidget. She wasn't saying any of the right things. Trust Josie to bring in the new shorts. He put out his hand to take the receiver.

'In a minute,' his dad mouthed.

'On a boat,' Josie said after a moment. There was another silence. Then . . . 'He's here . . . '

'It's my turn now,' Sean said, reaching for the phone. 'She wants to talk to me, doesn't she?' But Josie wouldn't let go. And there wouldn't be any time left for him. The money would run out. Still his dad went on shaking his head and frowning at him. Sean was getting desperate. At last Josie said, 'OK . . . Bye, Mum. Your turn now,' she said turning to Sean. He grabbed the receiver.

'Sean—?'

'Hi, Mum—'

'Sean, are you all right?' She sounded worried. Her voice was quiet and tense.

'Yes, we're both OK.'

'Is your dad standing right beside you?'

'Yes.' Sean paused for a moment, jamming the receiver tight against his ear. 'We're in France.'

'OK. Good. Listen, love, I may have to come out and look for you. Do you understand? Or it might even be the police.'

'OK,' said Sean.

'Only don't say anything, will you? To your dad . . .
I'd rather it was a surprise—'

'All right.'

'Whatever happens I'll see you both soon. And listen
. . . Take care of Josie for me. Stay with her, won't you?
She's only—'

Only little, his mum was going to say. But instead of
her voice Sean heard the dialling tone.

'Money's run out,' his father said, taking the phone
from Sean's hand. 'Never mind, we'll ring again in a
couple of days.' He smiled, putting it back on the hook.

Looking at him, Sean was almost certain that his
father had leant across and cut them off.

# 4

Sean wasn't at school the next morning. Tinker had guessed that he wouldn't be. No one said anything all day about what had happened. Sitting beside Sean's empty place, Tinker couldn't stop worrying about where he was. And then, at the end of the afternoon, just before the bell rang, there was a knock on the classroom door and in came a policeman; the same policeman Tinker had met the day before.

'This is Detective Constable Harding,' said Mrs Williams, their teacher. 'He's come to talk to you for a few minutes before you go home. So sit up everyone, please, and pay attention.'

There was a bit of shuffling and whispering, because no one knew what it was about, except Tinker, and then the detective constable took a step forward and cleared his throat and everything went quiet.

'Good afternoon, children,' he began. 'I'm here to ask you for your help. You see, one of your classmates, Sean Taylor, has disappeared, and so has his younger sister, Josie. You all know Sean, don't you?' There were nods and murmurs, and most of the kids turned round to stare at the empty place beside Tinker.

'Hush, everyone,' said Mrs Williams through the whispering. 'Please listen.'

'Well, yesterday afternoon,' the detective constable went on, 'both of them were collected from school by someone, and we're not sure who it was. All we know is that Sean and Josie haven't been home since. Now— what we're hoping is that one of you might remember

26

something—anything at all—that will help us to find them. We believe that they were driven off in a black car—possibly a Ford Mondeo—' He glanced at Tinker, who began to blush. 'Maybe one of you saw the car and might remember the registration . . . or if any of you saw who was in the car and could tell us whether it was a man or a woman, and what they looked like— well, that would be a big help, too.' He paused for a moment, looking round at the sea of faces, and then went on. 'So, when you come out of school today I'll be there, and so will Mrs Taylor, Sean's mum. Now that's the time you may remember something, because it was this time yesterday that Sean and Josie disappeared. Did you talk to Sean on your way out of school? Or Josie? Were they expecting to meet someone? Did any of you see the car—or see them get into it?' He smiled. 'It's a bit like *Crimewatch UK*, isn't it? I expect some of you have seen that programme on TV. So let's try to recreate what happened yesterday. All right? And thank you. Thank you all.'

As soon as he had gone an excited buzz of conversation broke out, and then the bell rang and everyone scraped back their chairs.

On the way out Tinker found Kate Armstrong walking beside him.

'You and Sean are friends, aren't you?' she said.

He nodded. 'It was me who told the police about it being a Ford Mondeo.'

'I knew that anyway,' Paul Donovan said, joining them. 'It was the car that was hooting, wasn't it?' Tinker nodded.

'You can't remember the reg, can you?' he asked.

Paul frowned. Then shook his head.

'Sorry. There was a sticker in the back, though. You know—on the back windscreen—like the signs they put up that tell which garage sold the car. I remember that because the stripes round it were the same colour as the

27

Wanderers football team—red and yellow.' He frowned again. 'I think it began with an H.'

Tinker squinted up the street to where the car had been, his face tense with concentration. He remembered the sign in the back too, now that Paul had reminded him. He'd been watching as Sean bent down to look inside the car. 'H' . . . red and yellow stripes, like a circus tent. 'H' . . . He screwed his eyes tight shut, knowing that Kate and Paul were watching him, and willed himself to remember.

'Hamptons,' he shouted suddenly. He opened his eyes wide and looked at them. 'That was it! Hamptons!'

At the same time as Tinker, Kate, and Paul were standing outside the school gates talking to Sean's mum and the detective constable, Sean's dad was just turning in at the gates of a hotel near Bordeaux in south-west France.

Sean had been in a daze all day, ever since the phone call that morning. He'd known from the beginning, of course, deep down. It was just that he wasn't absolutely sure. After the phone call there was no longer any doubt. They weren't supposed to be in France with their dad.

I should have gone when we were in the burger bar, he'd thought, as he followed his father and Josie along the harbour. I could have done it then.

It was too late to run away now.

Josie was skipping along the quay, holding her dad's hand. Ahead of them Sean could see Isabella standing in the middle of the pile of luggage. She held out her arms to Josie, who let go of her dad's hand and ran towards her.

'What did your mum have to say?' Sean's dad asked, waiting for him to catch up. Sean shrugged.

'Not much. Just asked if we were all right.' A warning voice inside his head was telling him to be careful.

'Come on, Sean! She must have said a bit more than that.' His dad smiled at him, all white teeth and dark glasses. Sean couldn't see his eyes.

'There wasn't time to say much.' He frowned. 'Josie had the phone for ages. Then the money ran out.'

'She must have been surprised when you said you were in France,' his father said after a moment.

Something clicked into place in Sean's head.

'I thought you said she knew.'

There was silence between them for a moment. The wind had sprung up and was ruffling his dad's hair. He ran his fingers through it, glancing towards Isabella and Josie.

'Tell you what we're going to do now,' he said, slipping his arm round Sean's shoulders. 'We're going to pick up the car from the rental office. Then we'll head for the hotel. You're going to love it there, old son, and that's a promise. For a start, there's a swimming pool . . . you and Josie will enjoy that.' He propelled Sean along the quay as he spoke.

'We've got no swimming things with us,' Sean said. His father smiled.

'Worry-guts! There are swimming things in the striped carrier bag. Wonder woman, Isabella is!'

Sean was silent. The sun had gone in and the harbour looked suddenly grey and desolate. They've planned it all, he thought. Everything . . . even the swimming things.

When they came up Josie was jumping backwards and forwards across the carrier bags, holding on to Isabella's hand.

'Is it done?' Isabella asked. Sean's dad nodded. 'Good.' They smiled at one another over Josie's head. 'Then we go and get the car now?'

They had driven along the coast to begin with. Sean stared out at the sea, hugging his school bag against his chest. If he half closed his eyes he thought he could see the English coast. Isabella was sitting in front with the map spread out on her knees; Josie was next to him on the back seat. She hummed happily as she dressed and undressed the teddy their dad had given her. First she took his tartan waistcoat off, then she put it back on again. The teddy had shoes, too. Before long one of them dropped on the floor of the car, out of reach. Josie began to wriggle out of her seat belt, stretching down to get it.

'You must stay in your seat belt, darling,' their dad said, half turning round. 'Don't undo it, will you?'

'I'm not,' Josie said.

'She's undone it already,' Sean said. Josie stuck her tongue out at him.

'Haven't!'

'Yes you have,' Sean said.

'Haven't,' Josie said, aiming a kick at him.

'Ouch!' Sean yelled. 'That hurt.'

Isabella swung round. Her eyes were angry.

'You heard your daddy, Josie. You must stay in your belt,' she said.

'But I want Teddy's shoes,' Josie wailed.

'Here, I get them for you,' Isabella told her, reaching down between the seats. Her hands were very white, with red painted nails. Like claws dipped in blood, Sean thought. 'There, now you sit down and do the belt up again,' she said, handing Josie the shoes. Josie snatched them and began to put them on the teddy. 'Josie—the belt,' Isabella said. Josie shook her head.

'Anyway, you're not my mum,' she said after a moment. 'You're not my teacher either. So I don't have to do what you say.'

Isabella went red, and for a moment there was silence. Then their dad looked quickly over his shoulder.

'Get that seat belt on again at once,' he told Josie. 'At once, you cheeky little mare . . . or I'll stop the car.'

Josie bit her lip and gazed glassily ahead of her.

'NOW!' he roared so loudly that Sean felt himself jump.

30

'Here, I help you,' Isabella said, slipping out of her own belt and turning round.

For a while after that there was silence. Then Sean saw his dad lean forward and slot a tape into the deck. As soon as the music began, Josie nudged him in the ribs.

'Anyway, she can't, can she?' she whispered. Sean shot a quick look towards his dad, but his mind was on the road. He looked at Josie again and very cautiously shook his head. They smiled at one another.

'I expect they're tired,' Sean heard his dad say. Isabella nodded, smoothing out the map and staring straight ahead, her chin tilted up. Josie started to hum in time to the music, dancing the teddy up and down. Sean closed his eyes, trying to remember everything his mum had said. After a moment he could hear her voice in his head.

'I may have to come and find you . . . or the police may come.'

The police. She was worried all right. She'd never have said that otherwise. But how would the police ever find them? France was huge, much bigger than England. How would they know where to look?

'Whatever happens, I'll see you soon.' She'd said that, too. Sean felt a sudden lump in his throat. He opened his eyes, blinking hard.

Josie had gone to sleep. Music often sent her off. Looking out of the window, Sean saw huge, brown winter fields with here and there a line of trees, their leaves lemon yellow and ready to drop. In the distance a grey town crowned a hill, the pointed church spire rising from amongst the buildings. Sean leant forward. He wanted to know where they were. But his father caught his eye in the mirror and put his finger to his lips, signalling towards Josie.

'Try and get some mileage under our belts before she wakes up,' he whispered.

'How far is it?' Sean whispered. Just then a sign loomed up.

'There—Direction Bordeaux,' Isabella said quietly.

Sean leant back again and closed his eyes, memorizing the name on the sign. BORDEAUX. Now at least he knew where they were heading. It was better than nothing. For a while he pretended to be asleep.

'Harvey—the phone call—'

'Not now,' his father said quickly. 'Little jugs have long ears.'

'*Qué?*' Isabella sounded puzzled.

'An English expression,' his father chuckled. 'They might hear.'

'Ah. But they're asleep.'

'Maybe.' Sean sensed Isabella turn to look at him. 'Anyway, the faster we can push on the better. I'd like to get to the hotel by four. What do you think?'

There was a rustle as Isabella picked up the map.

It's as though we're running away, Sean thought. But where are we running to?

# 5

For a time, later on that day, Sean forgot to worry. He even felt quite good.

It began as soon as the car turned off the road between the tall, white gateposts. The drive leading to the hotel wound its way between clumps of pine trees, their trunks flushed pink by the setting sun. Below the trees, grassy banks dipped and rolled like a green ocean. It was then, sitting forward in his seat, that Sean suddenly caught sight of the sea.

'Look!' he said, nudging Josie. 'We'll be able to swim.'

'It'll be too cold for the sea,' his dad said. 'But there's the pool—remember? And table tennis—'

'But we can go to the beach, can't we?' Sean asked.

'Me, too,' Josie chipped in. 'Can we, Dad? Please?'

'As soon as we've checked in to the hotel,' he laughed. 'You want to see your room, don't you?'

Sean nodded. Neither he nor Josie had ever stayed in a hotel before. They'd had a holiday cottage once, in Norfolk, but this was different.

'How many nights are we going to stay here?' he asked, leaning forward. He saw his father glance at Isabella. And then the car rounded the last bend in the drive.

'Look! Sean . . . Josie . . . there is the hotel!' Isabella said.

The building was large and white, with a flight of steps leading up to the front door under a green and white striped awning. Behind, the pine trees rose like a dark crown, and in front, where it said Hotel Europa, the flags of different countries fluttered on tall poles that were set in their own circle of grass. A man in a brown uniform decorated with gold braid had appeared at the entrance, and as soon as the car stopped, he came towards them.

'*Bien venue*—Welcome to the Hotel Europa,' he said.

Inside there was a marble floor, potted plants, and a long desk of dark, shining wood with a huge vase of flowers at one end. Beyond the plants, Sean could see groups of cane chairs and tables, a big window, and outside, green grass, tubs of flowers and in the distance, the sea. Behind the desk the receptionist was waiting for them.

'Taylor,' said Sean's dad. 'We have a booking.'

'Ah yes, Monsieur Taylor. We have your rooms ready for you,' she smiled. 'The suite for you and the two children, and next door a single room for Mademoiselle. If you would just sign here, and then Jean-Pierre will take your bags up to the second floor.'

'What's a suite?' Josie whispered, jiggling her dad's sleeve.

'Wait and see,' he smiled, winking at Isabella.

The suite turned out to be two bedrooms, a sitting room, and a bathroom. It was almost as big as their flat in London.

'Is all this for us?' Josie asked, her eyes wide. Her dad nodded. 'You mean—all of it?'

Sean was already on the balcony. There was a table out there with chairs round it, and below, gardens running down to the sea.

'Look at this,' Josie called from the bathroom. '*Three* basins!'

'Two,' said Sean. 'That's not a basin. Not really.' He pointed at the bidet.

'What's it for then?' Josie asked.

'You can wash your feet in it when you come up from the beach,' her dad said. Josie looked at Isabella.

'It's true,' she nodded. 'You can wash your socks in it also if you like.' She smiled at Sean's dad in the mirror, throwing back the rope of her hair.

The beds had white duvets and mountains of pillows. Sean bounced on his to test it. Josie curled up on hers and put her thumb in her mouth.

'Why not have dinner up here?' their father said. 'It's been a long day.'

'Can we watch television?' she asked.

'Sure—only the programmes will be in French.'

'French! Yuck!' said Josie, putting her thumb back in her mouth.

'I want to go to the beach,' Sean said.

'Yeah . . . the beach!' Josie bounced off the bed.

'The beach! The beach!' They both yelled.

'OK,' their dad laughed, holding up his hand. 'Here's what we'll do . . . first, the beach. Before it gets too dark. Then we'll go and see the pool. Then we'll see the ping-pong table . . . then we'll come back up here and have dinner. What do you say?'

'Yeah, yeah, yeah!' they chanted. Isabella smiled, a cool pillar of quietness amongst them.

'Coming with us?' Sean's dad said to her. She shook her head.

'You go. For now I unpack—and drink a coffee.' He nodded.

'OK, kids. Let's go!'

Down on the beach the air smelt of salt and pine trees, and the sea was silver and pink in the evening light. Out at sea gold tipped clouds had collected around the setting sun.

'That must be west,' Sean said. 'The sun sets in the west, doesn't it?'

'That's right.' His father nodded. 'Straight on for the US of A.' He pointed towards the horizon, one hand on Sean's shoulder. 'Go West, young man . . . ' he said in an American voice. Then grinned. 'We could go west if you like,' he went on after a moment. 'To America.

What do you say, both of you? Disneyland . . . the Grand Canyon . . . the Everglades.'

Sean stirred uneasily, scraping sand with the toe of his shoe.

'Can we go now?' Josie asked.

'Sure. Just the four of us . . . New York . . . Hollywood . . . '

'But what about school?' Josie asked doubtfully. Her dad twirled his sunglasses.

'Well, let's see. There are schools in America too, you know. Or better still—I could teach you.' Josie giggled. 'Dad!'

It's a game, Sean thought, trying to smile, too. But he was half afraid that it might not be. At any moment, he thought, it might stop being a game and turn into something he didn't want to hear. He wriggled out from under his father's hand and bent down to pick up a brown ribbon of seaweed, still wet from the retreating tide. It was as broad as his hand, smelling of salt. Sean began to run along the beach into the wind, waving the seaweed like a banner and whirling it round his head.

'Charge!' he yelled at the top of his voice 'Charge!'

He could hear Josie's voice drifting after him.

'Wait for me . . . I want some seaweed, too. It's not fair . . . '

But he ran on without stopping until his breath gave out.

On the way upstairs they stopped at the reception desk. Their dad ordered steaks and chicken and chips, a mixed salad, two milk shakes, and a bottle of red wine.

'And ice cream for the children . . . ' The receptionist looked up, her pen poised over the pad. 'And an English newspaper.'

'For the morning? Certainly, Monsieur. They are flown in each night.'

'*Daily Mail*, then.'

Back in their room, he said, 'Right, you two, go and bath while we wait for the food.'

'Can we have some of those bubbly things?' Josie asked.

'Yes—only not too much mess, kids, please . . . '

At home they always had separate baths now that they were both at school and Josie wasn't a baby any longer. But Sean didn't make a fuss about it. While the bath was filling he and Josie opened all the little coloured bottles and emptied them into the water until the bubbles reached right up to the top. In the bath, Josie shrieked as Sean swooshed bubbles at her. After a while he swooshed once too often and she began to wail, saying he'd put soap in her eyes. Sean climbed out of the bath and grabbed a towel, surprised his dad hadn't come in already to tell them to make less noise.

But when he opened the bathroom door he saw that the room was empty and in darkness. The door leading to the balcony was open, though. He could see the thin stuff of the curtains billowing out in the draught, making a ghostly bulge. Sean hesitated. Then he saw them. His father and Isabella were outside on the balcony, their two shapes looking like one shape in the darkness. They had their arms round one another, kissing, like on TV or something. Sean frowned, feeling embarrassment wriggle coldly down his spine. He'd never seen his dad kiss his mum like that, not even long ago, before they started to row. Behind him he could hear Josie beginning to climb out of the bath. He didn't want her to see. He slid softly back into the bathroom again and closed the door.

Josie was halfway out of the bath, rosy pink, her dark hair streaked against her head. She looked at him in surprise.

'Here, I'll dry you if you like,' Sean said, picking up a towel from the floor and wrapping it round her. He sat down on the stool and began to rub her back. Josie leant against him.

'Do you like Isabella?' she asked after a moment,

37

skewing her head round to look into his face. Sean shrugged.

'Dunno.'

'But do you?'

'She's all right, I suppose.' Josie wiggled her toes.

'She's quite pretty,' she said after a moment. 'But she's not as nice as Mum, is she?'

'Of course not,' Sean told her. 'How could anyone be as nice as Mum?' Josie nodded solemnly.

After a moment, she said, 'I don't really want her looking after me. Do you?' She stared at her toes again, frowning.

'I don't need looking after,' Sean said. 'I'm older than you. Anyway, I thought you liked her. You looked as if you did.'

Josie shook her head. 'That was just pretending,' she said, her voice small.

In the distance, someone was knocking.

'Coming,' their dad called. There were footsteps, then the rattle of the door handle.

'Food is here now,' Isabella said, pushing the bathroom door open and smiling in at them. 'And see, I have these.' She held out new towelling robes, navy for Sean and pink for Josie.

Their dad was setting out the food on the glass-topped table.

'Nice bath?' he asked as Sean came over and stood near him, tying the belt of his robe. 'And how's my sweetheart?'

'I've got a new dressing gown,' Josie crowed. 'Look!' She whirled round.

'Very nice—like a pink sugar mouse . . . Hey! Mind that bottle of wine. Better come and eat, both of you, before this gets cold.'

'Yum yum,' Josie said, bouncing down in front of her chicken and chips. 'I'm starving.'

Sean was hungry too. It seemed ages since their last meal. His dad had set a small table for himself and

Isabella, and pouring two glasses of wine, he raised his own to her in a silent toast. They smiled at one another across the table.

'I'm going to Emma's birthday party next Wednesday,' Josie said into the silence. 'She's going to have a conjuror. We'll be home by then, won't we?' She looked across at her father, a forkful of chips in mid air. 'Emma's my friend.'

Sean stared at his father. Isabella had put her glass down and turned her head towards the window. His dad had his hand on the bottle of wine.

'We will, won't we, Dad?' Josie said again.

Sean held his breath. After a long moment his dad laughed, jerking the wine bottle up from the table.

'D'you hear this, Isabella? I bring these kids to one of the best hotels in France, give them everything the heart could desire, and all my daughter can think about is some birthday party next Wednesday.'

Josie frowned, like a dog that won't let go of a bone.

'But we will, won't we? Because Emma's my friend . . . my best, best friend. And I have to go to her party.' She stared at him accusingly. 'We won't still be in France by then, will we?'

Her dad smiled then, and shook his head.

'No, sweetheart. We won't be in France on Wednesday,' he said. 'I can promise you that.'

Josie gave a little nod.

'Good.' And then, suddenly forgetting about the party, 'Can we watch TV now?'

Sean watched his dad cross the room and turn it on, clicking through the channels until he found a cartoon.

She thinks Dad has said we'll be back for the party, he thought. But she's wrong. He hasn't said that at all.

39

# 6

It was Josie who found the picture of them both.

She'd woken up first, and seeing something sticking under the door of their room, had gone to look. It was the newspaper her father had ordered the night before. Josie picked it up and carried it back across the room. She had meant to be helpful, only bits of the paper slipped out and landed on the floor.

'Now look what's happened,' she said crossly, looking down at the scattered sheets. Sean rolled over in bed.

'What's going on?' he muttered, opening his eyes. Josie was squatting on the floor between the beds.

'Look!' she whispered. 'It's us. Quick, Sean . . . look!'

'Us?'

'In a photograph,' she nodded, pointing at the page.

'How can it be?' Sean frowned.

'But it is . . . ' Josie said. He pushed back the duvet.

It was them all right. Sean recognized the school photograph they'd had taken earlier that term. He had his school tie on and Josie was wearing her tartan hair ribbon. Beside the picture in large headlines were the words:

## 'BROTHER AND SISTER SNATCHED FROM OUTSIDE SCHOOL'

Underneath in smaller letters it said:

## 'London mother begs for the return of her children'

'What does it say?' Josie asked, pulling at his sleeve.
'Hang on,' Sean muttered, still reading.
'I found it first,' Josie said. 'Tell me . . . '
'When I've read it,' Sean said, nudging the paper out of her reach. His eye raced along the lines of print.

'A distraught London mother tonight begged for the safe return of her two children, Sean (aged ten) and Josie (aged five). With tears in her eyes Ros Taylor (thirty-five) told our reporter how Sean and Josie had been picked up from school by a man in a black Ford Mondeo . . . '

'Me, me, me.' Josie's voice rose, cutting through the words on the page.
'Shut up, can't you,' Sean told her. 'This is important . . . ' and then suddenly rocked back on his heels as the door opened.
'Dad . . . ' Josie was on her feet first. 'Look, Dad, look! There's a picture of us in the paper—of me and Sean—it's the one they took at school—'
Sean saw his father's yawn stop just as it was getting into its stride. Then he was across the room fast and sweeping the newspaper out of Sean's hands.
'But I want to see it,' Josie wailed. 'It's my turn . . . '
'Be quiet!' he told her. 'And get dressed. Both of you . . . NOW!'
All at once he was wearing his worst look, just like the times when there were rows at breakfast and he was shouting across the table at their mum. Feeling the familiar sick lurch in his stomach, Sean watched in silence as his dad turned his back on them and strode next door, taking the paper with him. Josie's eyes were suddenly afraid. She reached for a corner of the duvet and held it against her cheek.
'I only wanted to know what it was about,' she said.

'I know,' Sean said. 'Come on. We'd better get dressed like he said.'

'It is about me, isn't it? There's a picture of us—'

'I'll help you if you like,' Sean said.

Isabella had folded up their clothes the night before and put them in two neat piles on the chest. Josie shook her head.

'I don't want to,' she said, her chin starting to wobble. 'I want to go home—'

'I thought I told you two to get dressed,' their father said from the doorway. 'Now get a move on! And, Sean—' Sean waited, the pile of clothes clutched against his chest. 'You're to stay here, both of you. Do you understand? Neither of you is to leave this room until I get back. I'm going to talk to Isabella.'

'Can I come too?' Josie asked, scrambling to her feet.

'No! You stay here with Sean,' her father said, catching her with one hand as she ran towards him and pushing her back. 'I shan't be long.'

'I wish Mum was here,' Josie said when he had gone. Sean didn't answer. He wished his mum was there, too. More than anything he wished that she would just walk in through the door and sort things out. But she was in London, hundreds of miles away, and they were in France. And now something had gone wrong with his dad's plans. That was why he'd gone off to talk to Isabella, and taken the newspaper with him. They weren't meant to be here, Sean was certain of that.

If we could just go home now . . . quickly, he thought, pulling on his jeans, perhaps then everything would be all right.

When he was dressed he went over to the window. Down below on the lawn a gardener was sweeping up the fallen leaves. Sean frowned, leaning his head against the glass as he tried to think. Suddenly deciding, he spun round and went over to where Josie was sitting beside the bed.

'You've got to get dressed,' he told her. 'Dad said so.'

42

He fetched her clothes and dumped them in a pile beside her. 'You can watch TV at the same time.' He went next door and turned on the set, clicking through the channels until he found a cartoon. 'Look . . . Tom and Jerry.'

As soon as she was sitting in front of the TV he went into his dad's room and stood beside the bed, staring at the white telephone.

It looked the same as an English phone. The only thing was that Sean didn't know how to ring England. On the flat bit of the phone there was a card under some plastic with a list of names and numbers on it. The top one said 'Restaurant'. Underneath that was the word 'Reception . . . 9'.

Through the open door he could see Josie starting to laugh at the cartoon as she tugged on her T-shirt. Sean picked up the phone. Then he took a deep breath and pressed 9.

In London, Tinker and his mother had just popped in to see Ros Taylor when the phone started to ring. It was Saturday morning and they were on their way to Sainsbury's.

'Hello,' said Ros Taylor. 'Hello . . . hello . . . who is it? Is that you, Sean?' She ran her fingers through her hair, waiting. But whoever it was had gone. There was nothing now except the dialling tone. Slowly she put the phone back on the hook.

'Who was it?' asked Tinker's mum. 'Was it Sean?' Ros Taylor shook her head.

'I don't know . . . we were cut off. Probably. Damn . . . why didn't I get to the phone sooner?'

'It only rang three times,' said Tinker's mum.

'He's trying to reach me . . . I know he is,' Ros Taylor said.

'Then I expect he'll ring back,' Pat Johnson said calmly. 'Maybe he had trouble getting through. Tell you

43

what—Tinker can stand near the phone while he drinks that Coke. Just in case.'

'Good idea.' Ros Taylor nodded. 'Would you mind, Tinker?'

'Just pick it up if it rings,' his mother said. 'Don't say anything.'

'Can't I talk to Sean?' Tinker asked.

'Of course you can,' Ros Taylor smiled. 'But after me. OK?'

Tinker went across to the counter and put his Coke tin down by the phone. Behind him, his mother and Ros Taylor went on talking.

'So you actually spoke to them yesterday?'

'Yesterday morning. Josie spoke first. She didn't say much. I kept asking her to put Sean on, but by the time it was his turn the money was running out.'

'But he said they were in France?' Ros Taylor nodded. 'What else?'

'Not much . . . he sounded scared. Harvey was right beside him . . . ' She stopped, glancing across at the phone again.

'He'll bring them back after the weekend,' Tinker's mum said. But Ros Taylor shook her head.

'I don't think so,' she said. 'He's sold the car, you know. The police found the other one down on the Solent. So the kids at school were right. It was a hired car they saw.'

Tinker stared at the phone, willing it to ring.

'And then there's the flat. It's empty. He'd paid the rent to the end of the month and taken the keys back to the agent. When the police went round yesterday, there was nothing there.'

'Oh, Ros—'

'The police are hoping that piece in the paper will bring a tip off,' she went on. 'Otherwise it will be like looking for a needle in a haystack. But I'm going to find them, Pat. No matter what it takes. I have to . . . '

Tinker pushed his specs up his nose, staring at the

44

phone. It wouldn't ring again, he thought. Not now. It was too late.

Sean stared listlessly out of the window as the big, white car headed south along the coast road. They must have been travelling for about two hours now, he thought. They'd stopped only once since leaving the hotel, to change cars in Bordeaux and buy some food in a supermarket. There had been no time for breakfast at the hotel. They'd left in too much of a hurry. Sean thought it was because of the phone call. His dad hadn't been pleased.

'You're going to get me into trouble, Sean, doing that,' he'd said, shaking his head sadly as he took the phone out of Sean's hand and put it back on the cradle. 'Is that what you want, son?'

'I was only trying to phone Mum,' Sean said. 'Why can't I?'

For a moment his father didn't answer, just stared at him, and the silence was worse than if he'd shouted.

'It's because of that bit in the paper, isn't it?' he said at last, sitting down on the bed and holding Sean in front of him. 'That's why you wanted to speak to her, isn't it?' Sean nodded.

'She worries,' he said. 'In the paper it said she was upset . . . ' He stopped, seeing the anger flash across his father's face.

'She shouldn't have done that,' he said, almost to himself. 'Why go to the papers with a stupid story like that? Snatched indeed! I love you both, Sean. You and Josie . . . you know that.' He gave Sean a shake as he spoke. 'You're *my kids*, aren't you?' He frowned, glancing towards the window. 'Now half the police in France will be hunting for us, and if we're caught I might even be sent to prison . . . ' He paused. 'You don't want that, do you?'

'Of course not,' Sean muttered. 'I just don't

understand, that's all. Yesterday you said Mum knew where we were—you said . . . '

'I know,' his father cut in. 'I know. Look, Sean, some things are hard to explain. But the truth is, your mum would never have let you go. You can see that, can't you? That's why I didn't tell her.' All at once he was smiling again. 'And that's silly because we're going to have a fantastic time together, all of us. Do things I've always dreamed about . . . I just didn't want it spoilt. You can understand that, can't you?' He looked at Sean, his head on one side, waiting.

'I suppose.' Sean nodded doubtfully.

'That's my boy,' his dad said. 'But these phone calls . . . ' He took a deep breath. 'And I'm sorry, but I have to ask . . . I don't want you to phone again—'

'Not phone? But—'

'Not yet,' he cut in. 'Not till the dust's settled. Just for a while. Promise me you won't . . . '

Sean frowned. He could see the bristles on his father's face where he hadn't shaved yet.

'How long?' he asked.

'A week,' his father said. 'Two at the most. Is it a deal?'

It wasn't fair, Sean thought angrily.

'Two weeks,' his dad said. 'That's not so long, is it?'

'I suppose,' he muttered at last. There didn't seem to be much choice.

His dad had given him a hug then.

'Good lad,' he'd said.

It hadn't taken long to pack up. While Sean's father went downstairs to pay the bill, Isabella bundled clothes into two big canvas bags. Sean stood, staring out of the window. The gardener was still there, sweeping up the leaves from the lawn. After a little while Josie came and tried to push in next to him, swinging the cord that worked the blind backwards and forwards in front of his face. Suddenly Sean couldn't stand it any longer.

'Go away,' he yelled, shoving her so hard that she fell

46

over, bumping her head against the chair. 'You're just a pest, Josie. Can't you see I'm trying to think?' Josie stared at him for a second and then began to howl. The next moment Isabella was in the doorway.

'Sean that is bad . . . very bad,' she told him, kneeling down beside Josie. 'Your little sister . . . you have hurt her. Bad boy!'

'Oh, shut up, can't you,' Sean shouted. 'What do *you* know anyway? You've got no right to tell me what to do.'

'Sean!'

He didn't care. Tears were beginning to prick his eyes, and with one more furious look at Isabella who had her arms round Josie, he stormed into the bedroom and slammed the door.

A few minutes later the door opened and Josie crept into the room.

'Go away,' Sean told her. Josie shook her head and sat down beside the bed.

'I hate her, too,' she mouthed at Sean. Then she put her thumb in her mouth. Sean looked at her in silence. After a moment he swung his legs off the bed and squatted beside her.

'Sorry I shoved you,' he said.

'It doesn't matter,' Josie said, in quite a grown-up voice. 'Do you think we're going home soon?' she asked after a moment. Sean shook his head. Josie was quiet for a while. Then she said: 'But I will be back in time for Emma's party, won't I?'

Sean didn't answer. Instead he began pushing his things back into his school bag. He didn't want to leave anything behind.

But as it turned out it was Josie who forgot something. They had got as far as the lift at the end of the corridor when she began wailing.

'Teddy . . . where's Teddy? He's not here . . . '

'All right, sweetheart,' her father said. 'We won't go without him, don't worry. Look in the bags,' he told Isabella.

47

'Under the bed, I bet,' Sean said when they'd searched both bags without success. 'I'll go—'

'The key's still in the door,' his father said.

It only took Sean a couple of seconds to find the bear.

It was then, coming back through his dad's bedroom that he spotted the newspaper. It was still on the bed, sticking out from under the duvet. In his rush to get out of the hotel his dad must have forgotten it. Sean's heart beat faster. Suddenly the newspaper seemed the most precious thing in the world. If he had that, the picture of him and Josie in their school uniforms, and the writing underneath telling about how they'd been snatched from outside the school, then he'd always be able to prove who he was, no matter where they were in the whole world. He picked the paper up, and folding it quickly in half stuffed it into his school bag.

He was only just in time. His dad was coming along the corridor towards him.

'Got it!' he called, waving the teddy. 'It was under her pillow.'

Now, staring out of the window as the car travelled on, Sean knew that he'd have to keep the newspaper hidden. Whatever happened, his dad mustn't find out that he had it. The trouble was, it was making his school bag too bulky. Next time they stopped, he'd have to do something about it.

'Penny for them?'

Startled, Sean looked up to see his dad staring at him in the mirror.

'You were miles away, old son,' he said. 'What are you thinking about?'

Sean shrugged, feeling himself beginning to colour.

'It's Saturday, isn't it? *Match of the Day* . . . '

'Is that all?' His dad laughed. 'I thought it was something serious.'

At midday they pulled off the road for a picnic. There were benches and tables under the trees, and in the distance the sound of running water. Sean could feel the sun hot on his back. Even the wind rustling through the tall grass felt warm.

His dad sighed, lifting his face to the sun and putting his arm round Sean.

'Nice,' he said. 'You, me, Josie, and Isabella . . . something to eat, something to drink . . . what could be better?'

'Look—there's a butterfly,' Josie said, pointing. She scrambled off the bench and ran across to the clump of tall grasses where it was sunning itself. Just as she came close enough to catch it, it floated away, up towards the pine trees on huge blue and black wings. Sean's dad smiled lazily, tightening his arm round Sean, and Isabella laughed. Watching her throw back the rope of her hair, Sean felt a wave of unhappiness. He wanted his mum to be there with them, not Isabella. Nothing seemed to make any sense at the moment, he thought, wriggling out of his dad's grasp and sliding off the bench.

'Where are we going?' he asked, stooping down to pick up a pine cone. 'I mean—where are we going now . . . tonight?' His father had stretched an arm across the table and was holding Isabella's hand.

'Tonight? Somewhere in the mountains, I expect. A motel, maybe. That suit you?'

Sean shrugged, throwing the pine cone up in the air and catching it. His father watched him for a moment, and then letting go of Isabella's hand, went over to the car.

'Here,' he said. 'I bought some postcards. Want to write one to Mum?'

Sean threw him a startled look.

'Now?' he asked. His father nodded.

'Then we can post it in the next town we come to.'

'OK.' Sean nodded. He put the pine cone down on the bench and wiped his hands on his jeans to get the stickiness off. 'What shall I say?' he asked, looking at the picture of fishing boats in a harbour. 'Can I tell her we're in France?'

'Just tell her you're having a great time,' his father said, handing him a biro. 'Then Josie can add a bit at the bottom.'

Sean bent over the postcard trying to think what to write. He wanted his mum to come and find them like she'd said she would on the phone, but he didn't even know where they were. Then he realized that she'd know by the postmark. Quickly he began to write.

'I'll address it if you like,' his dad said, watching Josie write her name at the bottom and add a row of kisses.

'I can,' Sean said. 'I remember—' His dad pulled a face.

'Better let me all the same,' he said, bending swiftly down to pick up the card. Sean watched him slip it into his pocket.

'Did you tell about us being in the newspaper?' Josie asked, looking across at him.

For a moment there was silence. Then their father swung round and looked at Isabella.

'Damn,' he said. 'The newspaper . . . damn and blast!'

Isabella's hands flew up to her mouth and her eyes were wide.

'You left it behind?' she said. 'In the hotel? Oh, Harvey?'

Through the open car door Sean could see his school bag propped up on the back seat. Feeling himself beginning to colour, he swung off the bench and headed for the trees.

'Where are you going?' Josie asked.

'To look for pine cones,' Sean said. 'Coming?' Josie nodded, pleased.

He would have to get rid of the newspaper now, he thought, starting to run, pulling Josie after him. Before they left the picnic place.

There were loos on the far side of the car park, Men's

50

on one side and Women's on the other. Sean waited until his dad had gone in and Isabella and Josie were in the Women's. Then, grabbing his school bag from the car he headed for the far side of the block and waited. As soon as his dad came out and began to walk towards the car, Sean made for the door.

'Hurry up, old son,' his father called. 'We need to get on now.'

Inside Sean bolted the door and opened his bag. Carefully he took out the double page that had the picture of him and Josie on it, folded it into four and slipped it inside his library book. It would be safe enough there for the moment. Later he would have to find a better place for it. On the way out he shoved the rest of the newspaper into the litter bin and emptied the remains of his packed lunch and a couple of apple cores on top of it. Then he washed his hands and headed back to the car.

Josie and Isabella were already sitting on the back seat.

'You took your time,' his dad said, looking up from the map.

'I was trying to get that stuff off my hands,' Sean told him. 'Look!' He held out his palms, still smeared with the resin from the pine cones.

'We'll have another go tonight,' his father said. 'Want to come in front? You can map read if you like.'

'OK,' Sean nodded, sliding on to the seat. He shoved his school bag down by his feet and took the map.

'The next place we come to is Bayonne,' his father said, pointing it out. 'We pick up the motorway soon . . . here. After that it'll be plain sailing all the way to the border.' He reached for his dark glasses and turned on the ignition.

'What border?' Sean frowned.

'The Spanish border, old son,' his father said with a smile as the car moved forward. 'You didn't think we were going to stay in France, did you?' He laughed. 'We've got an apartment waiting for us down on the Costa del Sol . . . that's where we're going, isn't that right, Isabella? To the place where the sun always shines.'

# 7

'Any news?' Tinker asked when Ros Taylor opened the front door. She shook her head.

'Afraid not, Tinker.'

He'd known really. If Sean's mum had heard, she'd have been on the phone to his mum within minutes, and his mum would have told him.

'Nothing then?'

'Not a dicky bird,' Ros Taylor said. She smiled. 'Do you want to come in for a minute?'

'OK,' Tinker said, trying to look as if he didn't mind one way or the other. In the kitchen he put the package he was carrying down on the table. 'Mum asked me to give you this,' he said.

'What is it?' Ros Taylor asked, turning on the tap and running water into the kettle.

'Mincemeat, I think,' Tinker said.

'Mincemeat?' She slammed the plug into the kettle and switched it on.

'They might be back for Christmas,' Tinker said after a moment. He pushed his specs up his nose, not looking at her.

'Maybe.' She nodded. 'Not long now, is it? Till Christmas.'

'Three weeks tomorrow,' Tinker said.

'Yes,' she said. 'Yes, I suppose it is.' She wiped her eyes quickly with the back of her hand. 'Peanut butter or Marmite?'

Tinker had been going round most Saturdays. Sometimes, after they'd had tea, he would wander along to Sean's room for a while. In there everything was just the same, as though Sean might walk in at any moment. The model was still on the table by the window, the one they'd been going to finish the Saturday after Sean and Josie disappeared. Tinker never touched it. That would have been unlucky. Only half done like that it was waiting for Sean to get back so that they could finish it together.

'You miss him, too, don't you?' Ros Taylor said, watching Tinker spread Marmite on his toast. Tinker nodded, then took a huge bite so that he wouldn't have to talk. He knew he'd never be able to explain to Ros Taylor how much he missed Sean. He just wished there was something he could do to help. But if the police couldn't find Sean and Josie it wasn't much use anyone else trying. After all, France was huge, about three times the size of England. They could be anywhere.

'Anything?' Tinker's mum called as he came back in. She and his dad were watching TV in the front room. Tinker shook his head.

'Never mind,' his mum said. 'Maybe at Christmas . . . I mean, they can't have vanished into thin air. You'd think someone would have seen them.'

Tinker perched on the arm of the sofa.

'Can I watch *Match of the Day*?' he asked suddenly, not wanting to think about it any more. Not for a while.

'Bit late for you, isn't it?' his mum said doubtfully. 'What about your homework?'

'Done it,' Tinker said. 'Did it this morning.'

'Anyway, I didn't think you liked football . . . '

'Let the lad watch if he wants to,' his father said, unexpectedly coming to Tinker's defence. 'All the other kids do, I daresay . . . isn't that right, Tinker?'

'Me and Paul think that United are going to win today.' Tinker nodded.

'Paul?'

'Paul Donovan—he's in my class.'

'Well, I fancy Forest's chances, myself,' Tinker's dad said.

'Forest?' Tinker had turned quite pink. 'Forest are rubbish. Everyone knows that.'

'I suppose that's what Paul Donovan says, too, is it?' his dad said.

'Not just Paul,' Tinker said haughtily. 'Everyone . . . '

'That's the first time I've heard him mention any of the other kids since Sean disappeared,' Tinker's mum said later on, when Tinker had gone to have a shower.

'Or show any interest in anything,' his dad agreed. 'It's high time he stopped pining, because I don't reckon Harvey's going to bring those kids back now. Probably knows he'd be in trouble with the law if he did.'

'I thought Christmas, maybe?'

'Not a snowball's chance in hell,' Tinker's dad said, shaking his head. 'If you ask me the lad's gone for good. So the sooner Tinker forgets about him the better.'

Christmas was coming. In the old town there were coloured lights in the streets, and the shop windows were decorated with Christmas trees hung with red and gold glass balls and sugared gingerbread shaped like stars. Every afternoon when the loud speakers were switched on in the square, carols rang out. The music drifted down the narrow streets as far as the promenade. Sean and Josie could hear it from the balcony of their flat.

'I remember that one,' Josie said, her head on one side. 'That's the shepherd one, isn't it?'

'While shepherds washed their socks by night,' Sean grinned.

'Not washed their socks.' Josie frowned. She'd forgotten the old joke. Sean shrugged. It wasn't like Christmas anyway, not here, with the blue sea and sunshine and the palm trees on the promenade. Sometimes, looking out to sea, they could make out the great hump-backed rock of Gibraltar on the horizon, and Isabella, leaning against the balcony railing of their apartment with her arm round Sean's dad, had told them that on very clear days, they would even be able to see the mountains of Africa.

'And when you see the Pillars of Hercules, then you know it is going to rain soon,' she said.

It didn't rain, though. The sun shone strong and bright every day and there wasn't a cloud in the sky. It had been like that ever since they arrived, five weeks ago.

Five weeks and two days. Sean had made a calendar which he kept rolled up at the bottom of his school bag. Every morning he marked off another square. People in prison ticked off the days like that, scratching a line on the walls of their cell. Sean felt like a prisoner. He and Josie weren't even allowed to go out alone. His dad said it was in case they got lost and couldn't find the way back to the apartment, not speaking Spanish. But Sean didn't believe that was the real reason. For one thing, he'd noticed that almost everyone seemed to speak English, and quite a few of the people who walked up and down the promenade actually were English. From the balcony he could hear their voices floating up to him, oldies mostly, who'd come to Spain for the winter sun. Later, in the evening, as the sun set below the rim of the sea, the Spanish people who lived in the town would come out to walk along the promenade, whole families together. The little ones would be with their parents, but the older kids whizzed along on skateboards or roller blades, or gathered in groups, talking and laughing as they leant against the railings.

Sean had tried to go out on his own once, about a week after they arrived. He'd taken the keys off the hook and was undoing the chain when his dad came into the hall and saw him.

'Where do you think you're going?' he'd asked.

'Down to the beach,' Sean said. 'I'm bored.'

'You're not allowed outside on your own,' his dad said angrily, snatching the keys out of his hand. 'I told you that.'

'But why not?' Sean said, suddenly obstinate. 'I do in London. I walk home from school on my own with Josie every day.'

'This is Spain, not London,' his dad shouted. 'And if I tell you it's not safe, then it's *not safe*. Do you understand?'

That was the day when Sean had first known for sure that he and Josie were prisoners. It scared him. But the worst thing of all was that his dad still hadn't let them phone home, not once, even though Sean asked nearly every day. At first his dad said it was too soon, that they ought to wait another week . . . then another week. And when that week had gone past and Sean asked again, his dad had other excuses. There was no phone in the apartment, and he didn't have the right change, or it was the wrong time of day, or he had other things to do. Before long Sean realized that his dad wasn't ever going to let them phone home. That was one reason why he wouldn't let them go out alone. He didn't dare to, in case they tried to make a phone call. Or run away . . . or in case someone recognized them and started asking questions. If that happened, his dad might be in trouble.

We ought not to be here with him at all, Sean thought. He had no right to take us away like that.

But what Sean couldn't understand was why his mum hadn't written to them. She must know they were in Spain because although their dad wouldn't let them phone home, he didn't stop them writing to her. Each time they wrote Sean had taken care to add their address. He'd copied it from a letter which had come for someone who'd had the apartment before them. Usually they wrote on Sundays. Sean wrote first and then Josie added a bit at the bottom, and when they'd both finished he always put the letter into the envelope himself and stuck it down before giving it to his dad to post. But it was five weeks now, and they still hadn't had a letter back. Sean was getting more and more anxious. Surely, he thought, it couldn't take this long for a letter to get to England and for his mum to write back. What he was really hoping was that his mum would come and find them, like she'd said she would. More than anything Sean wanted to be back at home.

At night he would lie hunched up in a tight ball, listening to the even sound of Josie's breathing and feeling the ache of homesickness creep into his whole body. He'd think about his room, then, with the model he and Tinker had been working on, his posters and books and the drawer where he kept his precious things. Sometimes in his mind's eye he'd move out of the bedroom and into the kitchen. His mum would be there, cooking something on the stove, or sitting at the table doing the crossword in the evening paper. Sometimes, no matter how hard he tried, he couldn't remember her face, or the way she smiled, and that really scared him. At other times he imagined that she was whizzing away from him at top speed like some crazy film, waving as she went. But the best times were when he imagined he saw her coming towards him along the promenade, walking quickly, running her fingers through her hair and searching for him and Josie amongst the crowd. Suddenly she would see them and hold out her arms, and they'd run to meet her and she'd hug them both so tight that they could hardly breathe and never let them go again.

Sean puzzled over Josie, too. She had stopped asking when they were going home and why they didn't go to school any more. She didn't even ask where their mum was now, or when they were going to see her. It was as though she had forgotten all about their real life in London and was content to let Isabella pet and cuddle her, to brush her hair and do it up with coloured ribbons. She spent most of her time helping in the kitchen, and had even begun to learn the Spanish songs that Isabella sang to her, chanting them over and over to herself before she went to sleep. Sean watched in silence, feeling left out and lonely.

Why doesn't Mum come and find us? he thought desperately.

About ten days before Christmas, Sean made a discovery.

Every Monday morning Sean's dad went out to make phone calls, because there was no phone in the apartment. Sean would watch as his dad put the letter he and Josie had written to their mum into his pocket, together with the stack of plastic phone cards from the shelf in the hall. After that he smoothed his hair in the hall mirror, winked at Sean and opened the door.

'Back soon,' he would call to Isabella.

'Can't I come, too?' Sean had asked at the beginning.

'Business calls, old son, very boring,' his dad said, shaking his head. 'You and I will go out later, eh?'

Then there was the thud of the door closing, the rattle of the key in the lock, and five seconds later the whine of the lift as it climbed up to their floor. Sean could hear the sharp 'ting' as the doors opened, and another whine as it began to go down. He knew then that his dad would be gone for at least an hour.

That was when he would fetch the newspaper cutting from his room, and locking himself in the bathroom, would sit on the edge of the bath as he read it through. Not that he needed to read it. He had learnt it by heart long ago, but just holding the precious paper in his hands and staring at the picture of him and Josie in their school uniforms helped him to believe that one day soon they'd be back home.

After a while he'd fold the paper up again and put it in his pocket. Then he'd flush the loo, and turn on the taps for a moment or two before unlocking the door. Getting the newspaper back to its hiding place in the lining of his school bag was the trickiest part. Isabella moved as softly as a cat, and Sean didn't trust her. He knew that she watched him when his dad was out and sometimes, later, she'd tell his dad things he'd done. He was always the one in trouble, never Josie. Josie was Isabella's favourite.

But that Monday morning was different. Sean had made up his mind to ask his dad again about phoning.

'You said we could . . . later, when the dust had settled.'

Sean saw his dad's jaw tighten.

'I'm afraid it's not that easy, old son,' he said. 'I have tried myself a couple of times, you know.'

Sean stared at him in surprise.

'You never said.'

'Well—I didn't want you getting upset. I was trying to arrange a time for you and Josie to talk to her—to your mum. A time when I knew she'd be in.'

'What did she say?' His voice sounded odd.

Bright rays from the morning sun slanted on to the balcony. His dad put up his hand to shield his eyes, then reached for his dark glasses.

'She wasn't there,' he said. 'No reply. Out, perhaps.'

Sean frowned.

'I don't understand,' he said.

'I know.' His dad nodded. He glanced down at his watch. 'Look, Sean, we'll have to talk about this again later on. I've got to go now . . . meeting someone.' He stood up.

'Can I come with you?' Sean asked suddenly. 'Then we could try again . . . you know . . . phone Mum.'

He followed his father inside, watching as he slid his jacket off the back of the chair and put it on, then ran a comb through his hair and patted the pockets.

'Can I?' he asked again.

'Can you what?'

Sean followed him into the hall. 'Can I come, too?'

He shook his head. 'Sorry, old son. Not this time. Later on. This evening, maybe, only I'm running late as it is. About an hour, tell Isabella.' He smiled briefly at Sean in the hall mirror. 'Post this for you, shall I?'

Sean had almost forgotten the letter. It had a postcard in it with a donkey wearing a straw hat. He'd meant it to be a Christmas card for his mum. It might get there in time. He nodded, watching as his dad slipped the card into his pocket.

When he'd gone, Sean went into the bedroom he shared with Josie and shut the door. He was going to get out his newspaper cutting, but first he wanted to think. He went over to the window and looked down into the gardens below the apartment. The man who worked there was setting out the chairs beside the pool. A breeze ruffled the bright blue surface of the water.

After a couple of moments Sean saw his dad come out into the garden and walk towards the gate. The gardener had finished arranging the chairs and was putting new plastic liners in the litter bins. Sean saw his dad give a nod, and then, as he reached the gate, he slipped his hand into his pocket. Sean saw him pull out the key. And something else . . . Curious, he took a step closer to the window, then almost instinctively drew back so that he was hidden by the curtain. At that moment his father looked up.

Sean felt a prickle of fear run down his spine. But his father hadn't seen him, and apparently satisfied that no one was watching, he tore the letter quickly across once, then twice, and throwing the pieces into the litter bin, he let himself out of the garden, locking the gate behind him.

# 8

Sean knew then with a sudden, sickening rush that all the other letters he and Josie had written had ended up in the litter bin too. His dad had only pretended to post them. All the time he'd been tearing them up and throwing them away. No wonder there had been no answer from his mum. She couldn't write because she had no address to write to. She didn't even know they were in Spain. No one in the whole world knew where they were. No one except his dad and Isabella.

And unless he could find a way to let his mum know where they were, she'd never be able to find them. He would have to do something. And he'd have to do it soon. Sean leant his forehead against the coolness of the window and tried to think.

He must find a way to phone home, and what was more he'd have to do it secretly. There was no point in asking his dad any more. His dad didn't want them to talk to their mum. With a kind of shock, Sean realized properly for the first time that this wasn't just a holiday. His dad meant to keep them with him always. He didn't want them to go home ever again. That was why he daren't let anyone know where they were.

The unfairness of it all swept over him. He knew how worried their mum must be, not knowing where they were, waiting every day for a letter or a phone call. If she did find out they were in Spain she'd take the first plane out and come and fetch them. Sean was certain of that. Just one phone call, that was all it needed. And then, perhaps, he and Josie would be home in time for

Christmas. If only he could think of a way to get out of the apartment.

When Josie called along the passage to say that Isabella had got orange juice and biscuits for them both in the kitchen, Sean was still trying to work out what to do next.

Josie was in her most irritating mood, playing Incey Wincey Spider up his arm and giggling. Sean tried to push her away.

'Stop it,' he muttered. 'Get off, can't you?'

'Incey Wincey . . . ' Josie began again, getting up and dancing round to the other side of him. The next moment her elbow had caught the glass of orange juice, which toppled over and crashed on to the floor.

'Was that you, Sean?' Isabella said, swinging round. 'Ugh! You are so clumsy! Now see what you have done.'

'But it wasn't me,' Sean protested. 'Honestly . . . Josie was mucking about—' He broke off, turning to look at Josie. 'Tell her, why don't you?'

But Josie put her thumb in her mouth.

'You have spilt all the juice, and now you try to blame your little sister,' Isabella went on, reaching for a cloth. 'Also this glass is broken, and who is going to pay for it?'

'But it wasn't my fault,' Sean began.

'Lies as well,' Isabella cut in, her eyes flashing angrily. 'I think it best if you go back to your room until your papa comes home.' Sean looked at Josie. Surely now she would say something, stand up for him. But she just went on staring at him. 'Go . . . go now!' Isabella shouted.

Sean pushed back his chair. He seemed to get the blame for everything these days, especially when his dad wasn't around. He knew it was because Isabella didn't like him. Not that he cared. He didn't like her either. Sometimes he thought he hated her for having taken his mum's place.

Later Josie came into the bedroom and stood beside him.

'It's not fair,' Sean said, without looking up. 'It was your fault. Why didn't you tell her it was you?' Josie wriggled.

'You were pushing me,' she said sulkily.

'Well, you started it,' Sean retorted.

Josie said nothing. After a minute she knelt beside him.

'Anyway,' she said, patting his arm, 'I expect we'll go home soon.'

Sean's heart gave a leap. He swung round, staring at her.

'Who told you that? Was it Dad?' Josie shook her head. 'Isabella?' She nodded. 'Go on. What did she say?'

'Only that Mum had gone away and couldn't look after us for a while,' Josie said. 'But when she got home then we'd go back to London.'

'When did she tell you this?' Sean said, catching hold of Josie's wrist as she started to wriggle away. 'Tell me, Josie. It's important . . . '

'I don't know. Ages ago. When we first came here.'

'And how did Isabella know Mum had gone away?'

'How should I know . . . Let go, you're hurting me . . . Ow!'

Sean held her firmly, putting his finger to his lips as Isabella's voice floated along the passage.

'Let me go,' Josie said, her voice louder. 'I'll tell.'

'OK, OK.' Sean dropped her arm. 'It's all lies anyway,' he said. 'Isabella just said that. Mum's been at home all the time.'

Isabella's voice came more clearly this time.

'Josie—where are you? Come—see what I have for you.'

'Better hurry,' Sean said bitterly.

Josie stared at him for a moment, then turned and ran out of the room.

On Monday afternoons Isabella went to the supermarket in town, taking Josie with her while Sean and his dad went swimming. Usually it was getting dark by the time they were all back in the apartment.

That afternoon, when they came back, Josie ran into the sitting room and flung her arms round her dad's neck.

'The Three Kings are there—they're there now,' she said, the words tumbling over one another in her excitement. 'Can we go . . . please, Dad? Isabella says I can go if you come too . . . and Sean . . . we must all go . . . please . . . please!'

'Hey, you're throttling me,' her father laughed. 'What is all this anyway? What kings . . . and where are we all going?'

He looked across at Isabella, who had appeared in the doorway with two carrier bags of shopping.

'Three Kings,' she nodded, smiling. 'In England you have Father Christmas. Here in Spain it is the Three Kings who bring the presents—'

'And they're there now,' Josie broke in again. 'In the square . . . I saw them . . . and you can go and ask for what you want for Christmas.'

'Wha-at?'

'Yes, yes.' Isabella nodded. 'The children go to the Three Kings, like in London Father Christmas is in the big shops—' Her eyes were bright with excitement.

'I see.'

'So can we?' Josie asked, shaking her dad's sleeve. 'Because they're there now . . . ' Sean could see the doubtful look on his dad's face. Already he was beginning to shake his head. 'Please,' Josie was begging. 'Please . . . '

He won't let us, Sean thought. He doesn't dare let us go out into the square.

But to his surprise Isabella was on their side for once.

'I thought it would be all right,' she said, looking at Sean's dad and beginning to pout. 'Josie will be sad, Sean, too, I think.' She gave him a little smile. 'And me, also . . . '

'You mean—you want to go as well?' Sean's dad asked, looking at her.

'Of course.' Isabella nodded. 'At Christmas we always went when we were children. It will be all right, Harvey. I promise . . . '

He gave a shrug. Then smiled at her, shovelling Josie off his lap.

'Better go and see, then,' he said, standing up.

Out in the square a platform had been set up near one of the fountains, with curtains around the back and sides and across the roof. Seated on the platform on high-backed chairs were the Three Kings. Sean saw at once that they were really three women dressed up in Eastern looking clothes and wearing false beards. One of them had stuff on her face to make her look like the black King, Balthazar. But Josie didn't seem to notice the false beards, and her eyes were round with excitement as she stared at the three figures on the platform. Their dad looked across at Isabella who was holding Josie's other hand.

'What now?'

In front of the platform there was a queue of little kids waiting for their turn to go up the steps. A boy of about three in navy shorts and a red jersey was up there now. One of the Three Kings had taken his hand and was talking to him.

'You want to go up and ask for a present?' Isabella asked Josie, who nodded, silent for once with the wonder of it all. 'Then we must stand here, behind the others,' said Isabella.

'You want to go up, too?' Sean's dad asked him. Sean shook his head. They were all little kids in the queue. 'We'll wait over there by the fountain then,' his dad said to Isabella.

Under the velvet black night sky parents and grandparents stood around in little groups, talking and watching the children. Mostly they were Spanish, but above the splash of the fountain Sean caught the sound of an English voice, too, and near the bench where he and his dad had sat down a man with a video camera was filming the children as they went up the steps. It was going to take ages for Isabella and Josie to get to the front of the queue.

All at once Sean realized that this might be the chance he had been hoping for. With all these people in the square, and in the dark, he might be able to give his dad the slip. His mind began to race. He could see a couple of phone boxes over by the newspaper stand, only he'd be seen if he went into one of those. There were others, though, down on the promenade. He could run there . . . and then come back to the apartment . . . make some excuse. Then he remembered that he didn't have any money. He didn't know the code for England either. But maybe he'd be able to find someone to help him. He could ask one of the English people in the square, or down on the promenade. All he had to do was run. Just run . . . His heart was pounding as he looked quickly at his dad. This was the moment. His father was watching Isabella and Josie. Sean took a deep breath and began to edge away along the bench.

Then, as though he had guessed, his dad turned towards him and put a hand on his shoulder.

'I wonder what Josie will ask for?' he said softly, pulling Sean back towards him and speaking into his ear. 'A bike, maybe. Do you think she wants a bike?'

Sean shrugged, disappointment welling up inside him.

'What about you? Do you want a bike?'

'I hadn't thought,' he muttered.

'Or some roller blades? I want you to have something you'd really like,' his dad said, squeezing his shoulder.

I shan't make it now, Sean thought hopelessly. It's too late. He could see Josie clutching tight to Isabella's hand, her eyes fixed on the platform. They were nearly there.

And then, cutting through the cloud of his disappointment there was an English voice, right beside them.

'Excuse me, but you're from England, aren't you?' said the woman. 'I wonder, could you tell us what's going on here? This is our first time on the Costa at Christmas, you see. Are those meant to be the Three Kings?'

'Sorry, my first time, too,' Sean's dad said, his voice rough.

'Oh.' The woman sounded disappointed. 'Only our friends don't know either. What about your son—does he know?' She looked straight at Sean. He felt his father's hand tighten on his shoulder. The woman was staring at him curiously. 'Do you know?' she asked. Sean opened his mouth to answer her, but his dad was too quick for him.

'We're just passing through ourselves,' he said. 'En route for Abu Dhabi . . . '

'Ah, you're in oil,' she exclaimed. 'Well, that explains it, then. I said to my husband it seemed odd that this young man wasn't still at school, seeing as they've not broken up yet at home. So—an oil man, eh? Fred would just love to talk to you about that I'm sure—' She looked round, searching the square for her husband.

'Some other time, perhaps,' Sean's dad said, standing up and pulling Sean up beside him. 'We're just off to see friends, and we're late already.' And gripping Sean's arm tightly he walked him quickly away across the square. 'Damned woman . . . ' he muttered.

'What about Josie?' Sean asked, as they turned down a shadowy side path between some huge trees.

'Don't worry, old son. We'll work our way back round to the other side. She'll get her turn all right. And then . . . '

Sean looked at him. Even in the dark his dad was wearing sunglasses, like a film star or something.

'What?' Sean asked.

'We may have to move on sooner than I'd planned,' he answered after a moment. 'There are just too many nosy people around here.'

# 9

Two days later, when Isabella had gone shopping, Sean and Josie were out on the balcony with their dad. For once Josie hadn't wanted to go. She was making Christmas cards.

'This one's for you,' she said, slithering off the patio chair and waving the card around to dry it as she skipped over to the lounger where their dad was sitting, reading the paper.

'For me? Thank you, sweetheart.' He laid the newspaper aside and straightened up. 'Let's see—a horse.'

'That's not a horse. That's a camel, silly,' Josie told him scornfully. 'With one of the three Kings—and that's Baby Jesus in the stable—'

'And that's the star . . . '

'Mm.' Josie leant against him. 'Do you like it?'

'I do,' he said. 'Very much. It might be the nicest Christmas card I've ever had.' Josie smirked, making patterns on the ground with her toe. 'And now,' he went on, 'I've got a surprise for you.'

'For me?' Josie asked, her eyes widening.

'For both of you.' He looked across at Sean as he spoke.

'Is it a present?'

'Not exactly,' their dad said. 'There will be presents at Christmas, of course. But this is different. A real surprise.'

Sean's heart began to beat faster. He leant forward. Josie was bouncing up and down.

'Tell us . . . tell us! Is it a puppy dog?'

'No, it's not a puppy dog . . . and it's not a kitten either,' their dad laughed.

'Tell us then,' she chanted. 'Tell us . . . '

'Keep quiet and I will.'

'But I want to guess. Is it a—'

'Shut up, can't you?' Sean cut in. 'Just shut up.'

Josie glared at him and stuck out her tongue.

'That'll do,' their dad said, lifting her quickly on to his knee. 'Now this is the surprise . . . so listen. How would you both like to go and stay with Isabella's auntie and uncle after Christmas?' Josie slewed round and stared at him, and for a moment there was silence. Shock waves of disappointment washed over Sean. Just for a moment he'd been so certain. Home . . . And now this. 'They live on a *finca*,' he was saying. 'That's like a farmhouse. Up in the mountains. There are horses and goats. Dogs and cats, of course. Puppies as well, I daresay, and kittens galore.' Josie had gone very still. 'You could learn to ride—'

'I don't want to go to that *finca* thing,' she said suddenly. She looked across at Sean. 'Sean doesn't either—do you?'

'I'm sure you'll like it once we get there,' their dad said quickly. Josie shook her head.

'No I won't,' she said. 'Why can't we stay here?'

Sean was staring at the ground. Ever since the English woman had spoken to them in the square things had been worse. His dad seemed to have become even more watchful, always looking over his shoulder when they were out, as though he thought they were being followed. And that wasn't the only thing. He'd been spending longer and longer away from the apartment, and at night Sean had heard him talking to Isabella for hours in the sitting room. He'd known something was up, and this was it. His dad had decided to get them away from the town. Down here, on the coast, there were English people everywhere. Sooner or later someone would be bound to recognize them. That's why he wanted to take them out to the country, miles from anywhere probably, some place where no one would ever find them.

'Why can't we stay here?' Josie asked again. 'I like it here.'

'Yes, why can't we?' Sean asked, rocking forward on the canvas chair. 'I want to stay here, too.'

'Sorry, old son, no can do,' his dad said. Josie was starting to make her pig squealing noise. He winced, scooping her off his knee. 'Why don't you go and fetch us some of those choc ices from the freezer?' he said. 'One for each of us.'

'Why can't we stay here?' Sean asked again when she had gone.

'I've decided to give up the apartment,' his dad said abruptly. He stood up and went over to the railings.

'Give it up?' Sean rocked forward. It was worse than he'd thought.

For a moment his dad didn't answer. The only sound was Josie banging about in the kitchen. Then he swung round. 'To tell the truth, old son, the money's running out.' He gave a sideways kind of smile, twirling his sunglasses in one hand. 'I've had to get a job—'

Sean stared at him. 'What kind of a job?' he asked.

'Selling property . . . down here on the Costa. Just for a while. Isabella's going to help me in the office. Her speaking Spanish will be a great help—'

'You mean she's going to work as well?'

'We both start after Christmas. Sorry I couldn't tell you sooner, Sean. It was a question of working things out.' He paused. 'So you see, with both of us working—'

'I think you ought to let us go back to Mum,' Sean interrupted. 'I want to go home.' He stared at the shiny blue and white tiles on the patio floor, not looking at his dad. 'I want to go back to London,' he said, swallowing. 'I thought that's what the surprise was. I thought you were going to tell us Mum was coming out for Christmas—' He stopped. Isabella must have come back into the flat. Josie seemed to have forgotten about the ice creams and he could hear voices in the kitchen. 'Why can't we go home?' he asked again.

'Hey, hey,' his dad said gently, sitting down beside him and sliding an arm round his shoulders. Sean shook him off.

'You miss her, don't you?' his dad said after a moment. 'Yes, of course you do. I know that. I think you miss her more than Josie does. Josie's always been my little girl—' He sighed. 'Honestly, old son, I thought you'd be happy out here with me—'

'But if you get this job we shan't *be* with you,' Sean burst out.

'It'll only be for a while,' his dad said. 'Just until I can get some money together . . . three months, maybe four. After that I've got other plans . . . ' His father was watching him, his head on one side. 'Your old dad loves you,' he said. 'You know that, don't you, son? And we're going to have a great Christmas. You'll see . . . the best we've ever had.' He gave Sean's shoulder a squeeze and then looked quickly at his watch. 'Good Lord, is that the time already?' He stood up. 'Got to go. I'll see you all a bit later . . . OK?'

He'll never let us go, Sean thought, clenching his fists. This is going to go on for ever.

There was no point in asking again whether he could phone. His dad would only make some other stupid excuse. He'd lied about the phone calls all along. He'd lied about the letters, too. And now he was going to take them up into the mountains, miles from anywhere.

I want to go home, Sean thought hopelessly. I just want to go home.

He heard the front door open and then close, like a prison door banging shut.

I must do something, he thought. But what?

After a while Josie came skipping out onto the balcony. 'I'm going to do a card for Isabella now,' she said, half to herself and half to him. Sean looked down at her. She was lying full length on the ground amongst the paper and felt-tipped pens.

'Why don't you do a card for Mum?' he asked suddenly, his voice low. He glanced into the sitting room. But Isabella was still in the kitchen and couldn't hear. He went and squatted next to her. 'Don't you ever think about Mum any more?' he asked.

''Course I do,' Josie said, drawing a purple line across the paper. 'Mum's nicer than Isabella, isn't she?' But she sounded doubtful, as though she wasn't sure any more. 'She never writes to us, though, does she?' she went on. 'And we write to her every week. That's not fair.' She drew a pink circle and put a purple blob in the middle of it. 'Isabella says she doesn't write because—' She stopped, her hand hovering over the box of pens.

'Because what?' Sean asked. 'Go on . . . tell me.'

'I'm going to use blue now,' she said. 'A blue and an orange.' She scrabbled in the box, not looking at him. 'Why doesn't Mum ever come?' she asked, after a moment, her voice matter of fact. 'Is it because she's away, like Isabella says?'

'It's because she doesn't know where we are,' Sean said, his voice hollow. 'That's why . . . '

'Didn't you tell her in the letters?' Josie asked.

'Perhaps she didn't get the letters,' Sean said. 'I don't think she got any of them.'

'If she knew then she'd come, wouldn't she?' Josie asked, turning to look at him. Sean nodded. 'Then why can't we phone her and tell her?'

'We can't do that,' Sean said, beginning to shake his head.

'Why not?'

'Because—' He stopped.

Why? Why couldn't they? All they had to do was open the front door, run downstairs and out on to the promenade. It would be all right this time. There'd be someone there who'd help them. Someone like that

73

English woman in the square. Someone would tell them how to make the phone call. They'd need money . . . Isabella sometimes left her purse on the side counter in the kitchen . . . the keys would be there, too. Josie had stopped drawing and was watching him. Sean was suddenly excited.

'You're right,' he said. 'We'll do it. Now. While Dad's out. We'll go together.' He straightened up.

'It was my idea, wasn't it?' Josie said, pleased. Sean nodded.

'Only it must be a secret between us. If Isabella finds out she'll stop us. So you won't tell, will you?' Josie shook her head. 'Promise?'

'Promise,' she mouthed. Sean was thinking fast now.

'Listen, you go to the front door while I get the keys . . . Hurry. And remember . . . ssh!' He put his finger to his lips.

Isabella was standing by the sink chopping onions. Sean could see her purse and the keys amongst the rest of the shopping on the counter. He signalled Josie to go to the front door, and walked into the kitchen. Isabella looked round.

'Hello, Sean,' she said. 'You want some juice?'

'There's something wrong with the loo,' he lied. 'I can't make the water stop running . . . I think it's going to overflow.'

'Are you sure?' He nodded. 'Ach, you are so clumsy.' She put down the knife and wiped her hands. 'OK, I go and see.'

Sean waited until she had gone out of the kitchen. Then he picked up the keys and the purse and ran to the front door.

'Hold that while I open the door,' he told Josie, handing her the purse.

He'd watched his dad do it a hundred times, but at first he got the wrong key, and by the time he'd found the right one, precious seconds had gone. He'd just got the second key in the lock and was turning it when he heard Isabella behind him. He swung the door open, but too late. Thrusting Josie behind her, she grabbed Sean, pulling him back inside.

'Let me go,' he shouted, lashing out. 'I want to go and phone my mum. It's Christmas . . . you can't stop me.'

'No!' Isabella told him. 'No, Sean. You are not to go out of the apartment . . . your papa has said so.'

She was shouting at him, but Sean hardly heard the words. All he heard was the awful crash as the door slammed shut again. Knowing how close escape had been, a kind of fury came over him and turning on Isabella, who had him by the arm and was trying to drag him back along the passage, he put his head down and bit her hand as hard as he could. He heard her scream, and then she was thumping his back, and through it he could hear Josie's voice.

'Leave Sean alone! Don't hit my brother!'

'Be quiet, Josie,' Isabella screeched. 'Your brother is a mad dog. See . . . he has bitten my hand. And he stole the keys and my purse.'

Afterwards, Sean remembered kicking her as she half pushed, half dragged him along the passage. But she was stronger than he was, and thrusting him into the bedroom she slammed the door shut and locked it from the outside.

'Let me out,' he yelled, hammering with his fists against the door. 'Let me out!'

'No! You stay there until your papa comes home,' she told him. 'Then tell him what you have done.'

'I hate you,' Sean shouted. 'I hate you. I'll hate you for the rest of my life.'

He hammered on the door for a long time, but Isabella must have taken Josie into the kitchen with her, because there was no sound from the other side. In the end he slumped down on the floor and buried his head in his arms.

It was dark when his father came to let him out. Sean had cried so much that his head ached.

75

'I ought to punish you—you know that, don't you?' his dad said, taking him into the bathroom and wiping his face with a wet flannel. 'Biting Isabella like that. Honestly, old son, I don't know what came over you. Why did you do it?'

'I hate her,' Sean said sullenly. 'What's more, she hates me.'

'That's a terrible thing to say,' his father said. 'You don't mean it.'

'Yes I do,' Sean said. His father sighed.

'You've really upset her, you know.'

Sean shrugged, not caring.

'You took her purse . . . and the keys—'

'I wanted to phone Mum,' Sean cut in. 'She wouldn't let me and Josie out of the flat.'

'But you know you're not allowed out,' his dad said. 'Not unless one of us is with you.'

'I just wanted to phone Mum,' Sean said again. 'And Josie did, too. What's wrong with that?'

'You're going to get me into trouble if you carry on like this,' his father said, shaking his head. 'You don't want that, do you?' Sean didn't answer. After a moment, his dad took the hairbrush off the glass shelf and began to brush Sean's hair, turning him round so that they both faced the mirror. 'Anyway, your mum's not there. I told you I thought she'd gone away.'

Anger flared inside Sean. He jerked his head away from the brush.

'That's not true,' he said. 'You just don't want us to talk to her. I bet she's there. I bet she's been there all the time.' His dad was looking at him now. 'I saw you through the window the other day,' Sean went on. 'All those letters we wrote, Josie and me . . . you threw them away, didn't you? That's why Mum never wrote back. She doesn't know where we are, that's why . . . You don't want . . . '

He stopped. His father's face had begun to crumple up like an old paper bag. He bowed his head, resting his forehead against Sean's hair. Sean stood rigid, gripping the edge of the basin, staring into the glass. He didn't care any more. Somewhere inside him there was a small, cold flame of triumph.

'I'll make it up to you, son,' his dad said looking up at last. 'I promise. I couldn't risk it, you see. It would have spoilt everything if she'd found out, and I so wanted us to be together. I still do. You understand that, don't you?' Sean didn't answer. His father began to brush his hair again. 'I will make it up to you, though. You and Josie.' He kept saying the words over and over again, and his eyes had a bewildered look.

But they were words, just words. Even at the time Sean knew that there was no way his dad could make it up to them. Not ever.

# 10

Tinker stared out of the car window and wondered how much longer it would be before they arrived. Going to stay with Auntie May and Uncle Jim would definitely be the best part of the holidays, and he was longing to get there. Of course his mum and dad had done their best to make it a good Christmas for him. He'd even got the mountain bike he was longing for. But Tinker had been glad when Auntie May, his dad's sister, had rung up and asked them to go up there for New Year.

Auntie May and Uncle Jim didn't have kids of their own, so they always made a great fuss of Tinker, calling him Timothy, which was his proper name, and making sure that he had his favourite things to eat. Auntie May cooked all her own cakes and puddings, and sometimes she made bread, too, so that there always seemed to be a smell of baking in the big, old-fashioned kitchen with its scrubbed wooden table. That was where they ate, and where Tinker and Uncle Jim played dominoes in the evenings. Given half a chance, the two black and white cats, Kitter and Katter, would be on the table, too, curled up asleep on top of a pile of freshly ironed laundry. The big old dresser was lined with different patterned plates, rejects from the local pottery where Auntie May and Uncle Jim worked. Auntie May decorated the tea pots and dinner plates and cups and saucers. You needed a steady hand for that. Tinker had gone with his mum and dad once to watch how it was done. But Uncle Jim's job was even more difficult. He worked at the wheel, making teapots and coffee pots and jugs out of the wet, slabby looking clay, his feet working the treadle while his hands guided the clay.

'We're all going over to Manchester for the pantomime,' Tinker's mum had told him. '*Dick Whittington*. And we may go to that big theme park as well. Would you like that?'

Tinker knew that his mum and dad were doing their best. But nothing they did could make him forget about Sean. They hadn't forgotten either. One evening just before Christmas he'd heard them talking.

'Two whole months and not a word,' his mum was saying to his dad. 'I tell you, I'd strangle that Harvey if I could get my hands on him. It's even worse for Ros with Christmas so close. Poor thing. She hardly dares to go out in case they ring. All this waiting is killing her.'

Tinker, who had been halfway across the hall, took several big, noisy steps and flung open the sitting room door.

'Steady on,' his father said. 'You'll have the telly over.'

Tinker had made a card for Sean with a picture of Father Christmas in a space rocket on the front. A couple of days before Christmas he took it round to Sean's flat.

'I thought it could go in his room,' he told Sean's mum. 'Just in case—'

He was hoping that Ros Taylor might have heard from Sean. But he could tell by the look on her face that there had been no news.

'That's really kind of you, Tinker,' she said, doing her best to put on a cheerful voice. 'How about on the shelf by his bed?'

'Yeah. OK,' Tinker said. 'Right . . . '

'I'll be in the kitchen if you'd like a cola,' she said.

In Sean's room Tinker went across and looked out of the window at the pigeons that were cooing and burbling on the opposite roof. Sean's mum had said to put the card on the shelf, but Tinker didn't think that was a very good place. He propped it up in front of the model they'd been making instead.

'I was planning to get him some roller blades this year,' Ros Taylor said, reaching for the biscuit tin and passing it to Tinker. 'And Josie wanted one of those special dolls with hair you can do.' She stopped suddenly.

'Do they have Father Christmas in France?' Tinker asked after a moment. He didn't know what else to say. She seemed to be in a daze that afternoon.

'Oh . . . Yes, I think so,' she said, turning with an effort to look at him. 'In France, yes, now let me think . . . in France the children get their presents on Christmas Eve. They'll like that, won't they? Specially Josie. She can't wait for anything.' She gave a little laugh and took a quick gulp of coffee. 'Of course, they may not even be in France . . . '

'But I thought—' He stopped.

'I don't know what to think any more, Tinker,' she said, shaking her head. 'Truthfully I don't. I just keep hoping, that's all.'

'Maybe at Christmas,' he said after a moment, pushing his glasses up his nose.

'That's what I think, too.' She nodded, her eyes suddenly bright.

But Sean and Josie hadn't rung. Tinker knew because Ros Taylor had promised to phone if she heard.

'And another thing,' his mother had said before they left. 'I don't want you going round to Sean's mum's so much next term. Your dad agrees with me. It doesn't do any good. You've got to face it, Tinker, Sean may not be coming back.'

But Tinker didn't want to face it.

'Bet you he'll be back by the beginning of next term,' he said.

His mother sighed. 'Have it your own way,' she said. 'But if I were you, love, I wouldn't count on it.'

For a while after they arrived at Auntie May and

Uncle Jim's, Tinker did manage to forget about Sean some of the time, and on the day they went to the pantomime he forgot about him for almost the whole day. It was only as he climbed into bed that night that he remembered. They'd been laughing and joking all the way back from Manchester, singing bits of the songs from the panto and re-telling the best jokes. Tinker had felt comfortable and happy, squeezed between his parents in the back of Uncle Jim's car.

'Home again, home again, jiggety jog,' Auntie May chanted as they turned the corner into their street.

'Hot chocolate all round and then bed, eh?' said Uncle Jim.

It had been warm in the car, but outside, standing huddled in the porch while Uncle Jim searched for the front door key, the wind was like a knife.

'Smells like snow to me,' said Auntie May.

'Snow?' Tinker's dad sniffed the air. 'Could be, too.'

'If the cats are in the airing cupboard, it'll be snow,' Auntie May said, rushing into the house with a shudder as soon as the door swung open. 'Kitter, Katter,' she called up the stairs. But there was no sign of them.

When Tinker opened his eyes the next morning one of the black and white cats was sitting on his chest and purring fit to bust.

'Kitter?' he murmured. 'Katter?' He never could tell them apart. And then opening his eyes wider, Tinker saw that the room was filled with white light. 'Snow,' he whispered. Apart from the purring of the cat it seemed as if there was no sound in the whole world. 'Snow!' Outside the window the street was transformed. Tinker grinned, shovelling himself back down under the duvet. It was like being afloat on an ocean of whiteness. With the cat warm against his back he grinned again.

'You'll not get home till the end of the week now,' Uncle Jim said as they sat round the kitchen table eating breakfast. 'All the major roads are blocked, no trains running. Nothing. The police are advising people not to travel. And there's more forecast for tonight.'

Tinker's mum and dad looked at each other.

'I'll need to get home by Sunday,' his dad said.

'Sunday?' his mum exclaimed. 'Jim and May will be sick of the sight of us by then. Besides, there's Tinker. He'll be bored to tears.'

'Timothy will be fine,' said Uncle Jim, winking at Tinker. 'Timothy and I have things to do, haven't we, lad?'

Tinker nodded happily. He loved staying in the big, old terraced house with its brown varnished staircase and the pitch pine bathroom that smelled of Pears soap. Auntie May and Uncle Jim still had linoleum on their floors, and slip rugs in the bedrooms beside the beds.

'They're called slip rugs because you slip on them,' Auntie May laughed, and her eyes crinkled up at the corners.

Outside in the shed there was a fez that Tinker's grandad had brought back from Egypt, and a Union Jack that they'd hung out of the front window for the Queen's jubilee. And on the upstairs landing the bookcase had a whole row of children's books with names like *My Lord of Waverstoke* and *Emu the Eskimo Lad* and the *Boy's Own* Annual for 1928.

It snowed for most of the day and on the TV news there were pictures of cars and lorries stuck under blankets of snow and stories about people being marooned with nothing to eat except one Mars Bar between three. Tinker and Uncle Jim started making a model of a sailing ship.

There was more snow that night, but the weather man on the news said it should begin to thaw the next day.

'We'd best get on with our snowman then,' Uncle Jim said to Tinker.

'Never mind the snowman,' Auntie May said. 'Get on with that model, why don't you? Don't forget we're all going out to tea this afternoon—with the Clatworthys. You remember them, Doug?'

''Course I do.' Tinker's dad nodded. 'Kevin Clatworthy's father had the ironmonger's shop on the corner of Fraser Street.'

'That's right. He's got a chain of DIYs now, has Kevin,' said Auntie May. 'And a big house up on the Crescent.'

'Well, they surely won't want us, too,' said Tinker's mum. 'Why don't you two go and we can stay behind.'

But Auntie May shook her head.

'They specially asked for you both,' she said. 'And Timothy. Carol says she remembers him in his pram.'

After lunch Tinker's mum put on the dress she'd worn to go to the pantomime and Tinker did his best to wipe the glue off his fingers. The sailing ship was nearly finished.

'Just the rigging and the sails to do,' Uncle Jim said, with a nod of satisfaction.

The Clatworthys' house was much grander than Uncle Jim and Auntie May's, with a large front garden full of snow-covered bushes, and a Christmas wreath on the front door, sparkling with red and silver balls and streaming with ribbons. Then the front door was flung open and Mr and Mrs Clatworthy were hurrying them inside out of the cold.

The sitting room was huge, with three sofas, a cocktail cabinet and a real log fire. There was a grand piano by the window with silver-framed photographs arranged on it, and everything smelled of lavender furniture polish. In the corner of the room Tinker saw a trolley all laid for tea and covered with a white cloth.

He felt pretty much out of things, perched uneasily on the edge of one of the sofas next to his mother. All the grown-ups were talking to each other, and he knew he was going to have to sit still for hours and not knock anything over or crumble cake or spill his drink on the floor. He wished he was putting the rigging and the sails on the ship instead, and maybe Uncle Jim did, too, because he caught Tinker's eye and winked broadly.

'Of course we only got back the day before Christmas Eve,' Mrs Clatworthy was saying. 'And, oh my, what a change in the weather. It was so warm there, you wouldn't believe it. All the flowers were still out, of course, and oranges on the trees, and the sea as blue as Scarborough in August . . . no more English winters for us, eh, Kev?'

'Would you like to see our video?' Mr Clatworthy asked, when the salmon sandwiches and Christmas cake had been wheeled away.

The video wouldn't have been so bad if Mr and Mrs Clatworthy hadn't kept stopping it to explain everything.

'Of course, out there the children don't have Santa Claus,' Mrs Clatworthy said. 'They have the Festival of the Three Kings instead . . . imagine that, Timothy. You'd have had to wait until the sixth of January for your presents, long after Christmas. And here we are— in the main square now. And look . . . look, there are the Three Kings and the children—'

'They're lining up to ask for their presents, you see,' Mr Clatworthy explained.

'See, there goes one now, up to the platform, and look . . . there are the others waiting in line. Father got some good shots here, didn't he? And look, there's that dear little girl . . . and an older boy over there with his dad . . . I expect he thought he was too old to go up, eh, Timothy—?'

Suddenly Tinker was on his feet, scattering crumbs all over the carpet.

'Stop!' he yelled. 'Go back . . . please. Wind it back!'

'Tinker!' his mother said, tugging at his sleeve. 'Hush . . . sit down . . . '

Tinker shook his head, scarlet in the face by now.

'I saw him,' he said, looking round at them all. 'Don't you understand. It's Sean. I know it is . . . Sean's there!'

# 11

Sean sat perched on a boulder staring down the hillside.

In the valley below the last shreds of morning mist were dissolving as the sun rose higher in the sky. Already he could feel its warmth on his back. Further down the slope Josie was crouched amongst a carpet of wild flowers singing quietly to herself as she picked daisies to make into a crown for one of the goats.

If he turned his head just a little, Sean could see the Goat Man sitting on an outcrop of rock near the shade of the olive tree, the herd of goats around him. He wore an old, brown felt hat and his hands were clasped round the tall crook that he always carried. He sat so still that he seemed almost to be a part of the hillside itself. But Sean knew that he was watching them all the same. Above, in the blue arc of the sky, kites wheeled and cried, sailing over the mountain tops on gigantic wings. Sean heard them without looking up. He had grown to hate the mournful sound they made as they circled so far above his head. It made him feel lonelier than ever in the vastness of the mountains.

He frowned, fixing his eyes instead on the track that wound down the hillside to the whitewashed farmhouse that belonged to Maria and Alonso, Isabella's aunt and uncle. From the farmhouse to the gate there was another track, broader this time, and beyond the gate there was a road, a proper road that ran like a pale ribbon around the hillside to the village, disappearing for a while amongst the red tiled roofs and then emerging again beyond the houses to begin its zigzag journey down the mountain. If Sean walked to the very top of the ridge he could see the sea far below, a glittering strip of blue beyond the line of buildings that fringed the shore.

Today was the tenth of March . . . ten days since he had started his new calendar . . . eight weeks and two days since they had come to live at the *finca*. There hadn't been room on the old calendar for even one more day. Sean had folded it up carefully and tucked it inside the lining of his school bag, next to the piece from the newspaper.

Josie moved further down the hillside, and the Goat Man's gaze shifted with her. There was never a moment when he was not watching out for them. Sean had discovered that the first day when he had wandered off on his own down the track that led to the road. The Goat Man had come striding after him, and shaking his head gently and clicking his tongue, he had used his crook to bar Sean's way and turn him back again towards the house.

'I'm not one of your flipping goats, you know,' Sean had muttered angrily. But the Goat Man, who didn't understand English, only smiled and nodded and clicked his tongue again. Sean understood then that he was to be their jailer.

'Why doesn't the Goat Man speak?' Josie had asked, on that first day. Everyone called him the Goat Man, even Isabella.

'My uncle the Goat Man cannot speak,' she said, putting a pot of soup down on the table. 'Haven't you noticed that yet? He *can't* speak. He is . . . how do you say? *Mudo*—' She made a gesture towards her mouth.

'Dumb?' asked Sean. Isabella nodded.

'From birth,' she said.

Each morning, after his dad and Isabella had driven off down the mountain to work, the Goat Man came to collect Sean and Josie from the part of the *finca* where they were living. He brought a packed lunch, which Maria prepared for them, and a big leather bottle of

86

water. The weather was growing hotter each day now, and there would be no more rain until winter, so Isabella had said. Beckoning to Sean and Josie to follow him, he would walk across the farmyard to the goat pen, clicking his tongue softly to the animals that were gathered there waiting to be let out. Then, leading the way, he would set out for the pasture, walking slow and tall amongst the sea of bleating white, black, and brown goats, tapping the stragglers with his crook as he walked, and turning every so often to smile at Sean and Josie who followed behind.

Sometimes, instead of going towards the mountain, the Goat Man led them down to the river. Those were the days that Sean liked best. Then he and Josie would dam the ice-green shallows, or launch sticks into the water to see whose would go the fastest. Once the Goat Man brought walnuts in his bag, and cracking them open carefully and handing the kernels to them to eat, he made a little fleet of boats with matchstick masts and paper sails, fixing the masts to the inside of the shells with a scoop of mud. It was down there, too, by the river, that Josie had rescued the little brown goat. It had become separated from the others, and going too close to the water had slipped between two huge boulders and become trapped, its back legs deep in the swirling green pool, its front legs scrabbling desperately to escape. Josie had seen before the Goat Man, and running across to the water's edge she had waded in fearlessly and pulled the little goat to safety before Sean or the Goat Man could reach her. Seeing the little goat scamper bleating back to its mother, the Goat Man had beamed wordlessly at Josie as he wiped her wet legs with his neck cloth and put her shoes and socks on a rock to dry.

'I saved the baby goat, didn't I?' Josie said, flushed with success. And the Goat Man, half understanding, had nodded and beamed again. Sean had never seen him smile so much.

But even on the best days the thought of escape was

never far from Sean's mind. He put up his hand to shade his eyes and shifted a little on the boulder, gazing round at the mountains.

All this space, but we're still prisoners, he thought. I can't even get as far as the village. He looked again at the road that twisted its way towards the cluster of red tiled roofs.

On days when he felt he couldn't bear it any longer, Sean told himself that he'd get up that very night when everyone was asleep and walk out of the house and along the track to the road, past the sign that said *Pension— Rooms to Let*, and through the gate. He'd just keep on going until he reached the village. There'd be someone there who spoke English for sure. Thinking about it made him feel better. But he knew he'd never do it really, because he couldn't leave Josie. Besides, the dogs would probably start barking before he was halfway across the farmyard, and then everyone would wake up.

Sometimes sounds from the village were carried across the valley and Sean would hear the school bell ring for morning break and the voices of the kids in the playground. After the second bell, silence would fall again except for the cries of the kites far above. Then Sean would imagine all the kids sitting down at their desks again, opening their books and looking at the board. The lessons would all be in Spanish, of course, but he wished he could be there just the same. The other night, in bed, he'd taken his maths book out of his school bag and, opening it at the last lesson he'd been on, he'd tried to work out some of the sums.

'You're an odd one, I must say,' his dad said, coming in and peering over his shoulder. 'Most kids would give their eye teeth not to have to do lessons.'

Sean frowned.

'It's boring up on the mountain all day,' he said. 'Anyway, I ought to be at school.' He gave his dad an accusing look. 'I'll never catch up now. Why can't I go?'

'What—here?' Sean nodded. 'But all the lessons will be in Spanish.'

'I could learn Spanish,' he said. 'I can speak it a bit already.' His father laughed and rumpled his hair.

'We'll see,' he said. 'Later, maybe, when we go to America.'

Sean's heart bumped. His dad was talking about America more and more now.

'Are we really going?' He frowned. His dad nodded. 'When?'

'Quite soon. I don't know exactly. Isabella's coming with us. Tell you what,' he went on, standing up and going to the door before Sean could say anything else, 'I'll see if I can find you some books in town— something more interesting than maths, eh? There's a shop that sells English books.'

'Josie, too,' Sean said. 'She should be learning to read.'

Josie wasn't happy any more. Sean was worried about her. Now that they didn't see their dad all day, and Isabella wasn't there to keep her company, she had a brooding, troubled look a lot of the time. One night, Sean had woken up to find her walking silently around the bedroom.

'What are you doing?' he whispered. 'Go back to bed, Josie, it's not morning yet.' But Josie didn't answer. She glided past his bed and through the open door into the moonlit passage. Sean sat bolt upright, then tumbled out of bed and went after her. She was still asleep when he took her hand and led her back to bed.

'I thought you were Mum,' she said. 'I want Mum. Why doesn't she ever come?'

'She will,' Sean said. 'You'll see. I expect she'll come up here to the *finca* one day and find us.'

'Mm,' said Josie, comforted. 'And when she comes we'll show her the goats, won't we? And the new kittens.' She turned on her side then, and putting her thumb in her mouth went back to sleep.

Sean knew that people only walked in their sleep when they were really unhappy deep down inside. He didn't know what to do. Perhaps, he thought, if Josie got ill they'd have to have the doctor, and then he might find a way to tell him that they shouldn't be here in Spain and ask him to phone their mum. Only if he did that, the police might come, and then his dad would probably get sent to prison. He'd told him several times that was what would happen if he was caught.

He's still my dad, Sean thought. I don't want him to go to prison, but I don't want to stay here either. And I don't want to go to America. I just want to go home.

He needed a plan, Sean thought desperately, a proper plan that would work. And he must think of something soon. If their dad really took them to America, they'd be thousands and thousands of miles from home, and it would be even more difficult to get back.

Perhaps if Josie and I ran away, Sean thought. We could get up very early one morning and creep out. Then if we could hide somewhere, somewhere in the village . . . if Josie could walk that far, then find somebody to help us. All we'd have to do would be to make a phone call and Mum would come and get us. And if we didn't say where Dad was, if we didn't tell, then he couldn't get in trouble. I'd have to tell Josie first, of course, and what if she blurted it all out . . . and . . . He looked down the hillside at her. No . . . that's no good.

It was the same most days. Sean kept making plans, but they were never any good.

He eased himself further up the boulder, watching the traffic on the road, far below. The cars looked like coloured beetles crawling round the side of the mountain, some coming up towards the village and some going down to the coast. The bigger beetles were buses and trucks. He shaded his eyes, following the course of a small, green car that was climbing towards the village. The next moment it had disappeared amongst the houses, and Sean guessed that he'd seen the last of it. Nothing came up the road to the farm, except the truck that brought the animal feed once a fortnight.

And then, to his surprise, it appeared again. He sat upright, shading his eyes against the brightness of the sun, and watched it as it moved steadily along the road that led towards the farm.

It's going to the quarry, he thought. There was nothing else further up the mountain, beyond the farm. But as it came closer it began to slow down, and then, to Sean's astonishment, it actually stopped right beside the gate. A figure climbed out and opened the gate, then climbed back into the car and drove through; got out again and closed the gate. Excitedly, Sean stood up, scrambling for a firm foothold on the boulder, and stared down at the car as it bumped slowly up the track and into the farmyard.

'What is it?' Josie asked, looking up at him.

'A car,' Sean said. 'Come and see.'

He could feel the knot of excitement in his stomach. Catching the importance of the moment, Josie jumped up, scattering her lapful of flowers on to the grass, and ran towards him.

'Look,' he said, helping her up. 'See . . . down there . . . Someone's come.'

# 12

Side by side they waited on the rock.

After a moment they saw Maria come out of the farmhouse and cross the yard. Then the car door swung open, and someone wearing a straw hat climbed out. The two stood talking for a little while, and then Maria nodded and pointed towards the empty apartment, directly above theirs.

'Who is it?' Josie whispered.

'I don't know,' Sean frowned. 'But whoever it is I think they might be coming to stay. Look . . . '

Maria had fetched the keys from the farmhouse and was leading the stranger up the flight of stone steps. She opened the door, and they disappeared inside. A minute later, Sean and Josie saw Maria throw open the long windows and fasten back the shutters. For a few moments the two figures were framed against the open window like dolls in a doll's house. Then they disappeared inside.

'Do you think—' Josie began.

'Hang on,' Sean interrupted, pointing.

They had come out of the house now, and back down the steps. The stranger was waving an arm towards the mountains and they saw Maria nod. They talked for a while longer. Then the stranger went across to the car and began to take luggage out of the boot.

'That means he's staying,' Josie said.

'I think you're right,' Sean nodded.

For the first time in weeks he felt a flicker of hope.

He put his arm around Josie to steady her on the rock

and looked across at the Goat Man. He had been watching as well, and now he was looking at them, and Sean could see that his face was sad. You could never tell what the Goat Man was thinking, of course, because he didn't speak, but lately Sean had felt that he understood how much they longed to leave the mountain. Things had changed since the day Josie rescued the little goat. Perhaps he knew that their real home was far away and not in Spain at all, and that was why he sometimes gave them such sad and thoughtful looks. All at once, he stood up, and nodding to them to follow him, he strode off along the path, his long crook tap-tapping amongst the bleating goats.

'Who do you think it is?' Josie asked again as they ran to catch up with him.

'I don't know,' Sean told her.

He turned to look back down the mountain. Already the farmhouse was hidden from view. But still Sean could feel the flicker of hope.

That day was Saturday, and his father and Isabella were back earlier than usual. He must have been looking out for them because as they came down the path between the olive trees that afternoon, he suddenly appeared, walking quickly towards them.

'Somebody's come,' Josie called out. 'Sean and me saw the car.'

'Quizzy monkeys,' he smiled.

'Who is it, who is it?' Josie was leaping up and down amongst the goats. 'Tell us. We want to know.'

'She's an American, if you must know,' he said, lifting her up and giving her a kiss.

'She?' Josie twisted round to look into his face.

'We thought it was a man,' Sean explained, seeing his father look across at him. He gave a little shake of his head, setting Josie back on the ground again.

'American,' he said. 'She's come here to paint.'

'An artist?' Sean asked.

'Seems so,' his dad nodded. 'She's been ill, apparently.

Now all she wants is peace and quiet. So that means you two are absolutely not to disturb her. Do you understand?'

'We'll be as quiet as mice,' Josie said. 'Won't we, Sean?'

Sean nodded, trying to look bored so as to hide his excitement. If the visitor was American that meant she would speak English.

'Quieter than mice,' their dad said. 'Mice can be quite noisy. Especially at night.'

'You mean they stamp around in big boots?' Josie giggled. She stamped around a bit and their father laughed.

'No, but seriously, kids,' he went on. 'You will have to be extra quiet for a while. Just keep out of her way, that's all.'

'OK,' Josie nodded. 'We will.'

But Sean said nothing. He could see that his dad was afraid the American might start asking awkward questions, like the English woman had the night they'd gone to see the Three Kings. That was why he wanted to keep them away from her. Sean knew he'd have to be careful, not look as though he cared.

They were halfway across the farmyard when she came out on to her balcony. Looking up Sean had an impression of a face seamed with lines, and a large nose . . . Like a big bird, he thought. She was wearing a blue checked shirt over jeans, and the same straw hat. Looking down at them she nodded

'*Buenas tardes*,' she said in a deep voice.

'*Buenas tardes, señora*,' Sean's dad answered, and before Josie could say anything, he pushed the door open with his foot and propelled her inside, looking over his shoulder to make certain that Sean was following.

'She probably thinks we're Spanish,' Josie said with a giggle as soon as the door was shut.

'Maybe she does,' their dad nodded. 'Now—how about going down to the village for supper tonight . . . *patatas fritas*, maybe?'

'Chips,' said Josie. 'Mm.'

94

In the restaurant their dad ordered pizza and chips all round, but when the pizzas came they were flabby and the onion was only half cooked. Sean couldn't eat more than a few mouthfuls of his. He watched his dad and Isabella holding hands across the table, hating the way they twined their fingers together. Josie didn't like it either. She tried to make them play the pile of hands game, going red in the face as it went faster and faster, and shrieking with laughter when it was her turn to pull her hand out from the bottom of the pile. Sean shook his head and wouldn't play. All he wanted was to be alone so that he could work on his plan. Somehow, he must find a way to talk to the American lady without his dad or Isabella finding out. And it must be soon. She might only stay at the *finca* for a few days. This could be their only chance to get help.

'You're very quiet tonight, old son,' his father said, putting an arm round his shoulders as they walked back to the car. 'Anything up?'

Sean shook his head. But his dad seemed to want to talk.

'You don't much like being up at the *finca*, do you?' he asked after a moment, studying Sean's face.

'Not really,' said Sean. 'It's boring. Why can't we go to school? We ought to . . . Josie and me.'

'I know, I know,' his dad said. He sighed. 'I've hated to leave you like this, believe me. But it's not for much longer. Things will be better soon, you'll see.'

Sean frowned. 'What do you mean—it's not for much longer?'

'Just that we shan't be at the *finca* for much longer,' his dad said. 'That's all.'

'But—'

'No more questions.' He gave Sean's shoulder a squeeze. 'Just trust me, eh? And tomorrow,' he went on, 'we'll go to the coast . . . take a picnic lunch and spend all day at the beach.'

Later, as he came out of the bathroom on his way to bed, Sean heard his dad and Isabella talking.

'Don't worry, Harvey,' Isabella was saying, her voice low. 'It's only for a week. She'll hardly see the kids. And Maria needs the money.'

'Of course. I wish they'd waited just a little longer, that's all. It's only another couple of weeks before we leave for the States. Maybe less. I don't want anything to go wrong.'

'It won't,' Isabella interrupted. 'I will arrange it all. You will see. She won't guess anything. Don't you trust me?' she asked after a moment. And Sean, leaning against the door jamb, imagined how she was looking at his dad, smiling the slow, sweet smile that he had grown to hate.

'Of course I do,' his dad replied softly. 'Come here . . . '

There was a creak, as though Isabella was crossing the room, and Sean took his hand off the door jamb and crept into the bedroom.

Josie was in bed looking at one of the old Peter and Jane reading books their dad had brought back for her.

'I can do this page,' she told him. 'Listen. "Peter and Jane play with the ball. Spot plays with the ball, too." See . . . I can.'

'Yah, yah,' Sean said, climbing into bed. Josie looked across at him.

'What's wrong?' she asked.

Sean wanted to tell her. He wanted to explain that their dad was going to take them to America and that Isabella was coming too and that they'd probably never see their mum again. But the words wouldn't come. Josie was still looking at him as though she knew something was up. Sean shook his head.

'Nothing's wrong,' he muttered. 'I feel sick. That's all.'

He rolled over on to his side. After a moment Josie went on reading.

' "Spot likes the ball. Peter and Jane like Spot . . . " '

Josie had been all right when they'd tried to get out of the flat to phone, Sean thought. She'd stood up for him to Isabella, too. But even so he wasn't sure if he could trust her not to blurt things out by mistake. He couldn't risk that. Not now. No. Somehow he would have to find a way to talk to the American on his own, before it was too late.

The next day was Sunday, and they didn't see the American lady all day. By Monday evening, Sean still hadn't seen her. All he had found out was that her name was Mrs Kauffman, because Maria had told them so.

'Señora Kauffman asleep,' she had said to Josie in a fierce whisper on Monday morning, as Josie started to sing. 'You quiet, nah?'

In the days that followed it seemed to Sean that the Goat Man collected them earlier than usual and kept them out on the hillside even longer. Sean could do nothing but watch and wait, charting Mrs Kauffman's day. By Wednesday he had worked it out. She got up late, after they had gone out with the Goat Man, and stayed in the upstairs apartment until the afternoon. Then, when siesta time was over, she would walk up the mountain, or down to the river with her painting things and stay there until the light faded. In the evening, the scent of barbecued meat drifted down from the flat roof, so Sean guessed that she sat up there on her own in the evening, cooking and eating her dinner.

By Thursday Sean was growing desperate. Isabella had said that Mrs Kauffman had come for a week. There were only two more days to go.

And then, in the middle of Thursday night, it happened.

At first when he woke up Sean thought it was morning. It took him a moment to realize that the brightness was the moon shining in at the open window with a light so cold and clear that he could have read a book by it. But there was something else.

Something had woken him. He sat up. And then he

saw that the door was wide open and Josie's bed was empty.

He was out of bed in an instant and padding softly towards the door. But there was no sign of her in the passage, and she wasn't in the bathroom either. He could hear his dad snoring as he tiptoed past his door. Sean frowned. There seemed to be a coolness around his ankles, and when he reached the living room he saw why. The front door was wide open. Somehow Josie must have managed to slide back the bolt.

Outside the farmyard was bathed in moonlight. Sean saw her at once. She was halfway up the flight of stone steps that led to Mrs Kauffman's apartment. He saw something else as well. Mrs Kauffman was on the balcony, watching. As soon as she saw Sean come through the door she held up her hand to him, and then, as their eyes met, put her finger to her lips. Sean nodded. The steps had no railing. If Josie was startled out of her sleep now she might stumble and fall down into the yard.

'She's asleep,' he whispered. Mrs Kauffman nodded.

'Don't waken her,' she whispered back. Sean nodded. Keeping to the outside edge, he began to climb the steps behind Josie.

'I'll go open the door,' Mrs Kauffman said softly, and disappeared into the darkened room.

Josie kept going. She was almost at the top step, the most dangerous part of all, when Sean saw the door opening. One more step, and then Mrs Kauffman had put out her hand and taken Josie gently by the wrist. Sean raced up the last few steps and took her other hand.

'Thank you,' he whispered. 'She'll be OK now.'

'You'd better get her back to bed,' Mrs Kauffman said. Then, as Sean began to lead Josie down the steps, 'You're English . . . ' Sean nodded. 'I had you down as Spanish.' She gave him a puzzled look. Not daring to speak again in case he woke Josie up, Sean stopped, staring helplessly up at Mrs Kauffman. As though sensing that there was more to say, she took a step forward. 'Come visit me tomorrow,' she said. 'I'd like that . . . '

He had to get Josie back to bed. But by tomorrow Sean knew it would be too late.

'No! Wait!' he called out softly as she turned to go. 'Please—wait! I'm coming back.'

His heart was banging against his ribs. At any moment the dogs might start barking, or his dad might wake up. But at last he had made up his mind. He knew now what he was going to do . . . if only she would wait . . . if there was enough time. Carefully he led Josie back into the house. For one heart-stopping moment the snoring broke off as they passed his dad's door. Then Sean heard it start again. A moment later Josie was back in bed. Turning on her side she put her thumb in her mouth.

Sean reached under his own bed for his school bag and felt in the lining for the precious piece of newspaper. Then, grabbing a felt-tipped pen from the shelf he wrote 'PLEASE HELP US' in big letters at the top of the page.

If she had gone inside again he'd push it under the door, he thought as he ran.

But Mrs Kauffman was still standing there. Sean raced up the steps and thrust the paper into her hands. And as he turned to go he saw the light come on in his dad's room.

He was down the steps again in a flash, and moving far too fast to notice that someone else was watching. On the other side of the farmyard, almost hidden in the shadow of the barn door, stood the tall figure of the Goat Man.

'Sean! What's going on?' His dad was dragging on his bathrobe as he came towards him. 'Where the devil have you been?'

'It was Josie,' Sean began, taking a couple of steps into the living room. 'She was walking in her sleep—'

'What?'

'The door was open . . . I had to fetch her in from the yard. It's OK, I've taken her back to bed.'

His dad grabbed him, looking into his face.

'I don't believe you. This is some story, isn't it?' His eyes were wild.

Sean shook him off.

'She is back in bed,' he said angrily. 'Look for yourself if you don't believe me. Anyway, it's not the first time . . . she quite often walks in her sleep—'

'Why didn't you tell me this before?'

Sean shrugged. 'What's the point? She wants Mum, that's all. And you won't let us go home—'

'Sean!'

'Well, it's true, isn't it? You haven't even let us phone . . . not once . . . not even at Christmas—'

'That'll do,' his father interrupted. 'We've been over and over this. I couldn't let you phone—you must understand that.' Sean didn't answer. 'Anyway, it's the middle of the night. You'd better go back to bed. And this time, just stay there. D'you hear me?' He took hold of Sean's arm and began pushing him towards the passage. Sean wrenched himself free, anger flaring inside him.

'Fine,' he said. 'So next time Josie walks in her sleep, I'll just let her go, shall I? I won't try to stop her, not even if she's at the top of a flight of steps like she was just now. I'll just let her fall off and hurt herself, perhaps die, and I won't care . . . '

His dad caught hold of him again.

'Hey, hey! What is all this?' Suddenly he looked worried. 'Is this true? Did you really stop her falling?'

'I told you,' Sean answered. All at once he was afraid in case he'd said too much. Supposing his dad started asking questions. Instead he shot him another worried look.

'I'd never forgive myself if anything happened to Josie,' he said. 'You know that, Sean. I'm sorry I said what I did. I just wish you'd told me about this sooner. Why didn't you?'

'Mum asked me to look after Josie,' he muttered. 'So I have done. That's all.'

His father pulled a face.

'All right. Only next time, wake me. Understand?'

'OK.' Sean nodded. He wanted to get away now. 'I'm going back to bed,' he said.

'Sure . . . good idea.' His dad nodded. 'I'll just come and make sure Josie's all right . . . and, Sean . . . thanks.'

Back in bed he curled up in a ball and pulled the sheet over his head.

He'd got away with it, he thought. His dad hadn't guessed. By this time she would have read the piece about them in the newspaper. He'd done everything he could, Sean thought. It was up to Mrs Kauffman now.

# 13

Ros Taylor rang the bell and waited, shading her eyes against the sun as she looked up at the tall, creeper-covered house. Beside the path the red flowers on the hibiscus bush were just coming into bloom. It would be different when she got back home, she thought. Nothing but grey skies and rain.

Inside, the secretary led the way along the passage and, pushing open the dark, wooden door, showed her into the Consul's office. He stood up and came round the desk towards her, a tall man, his face tanned by the Spanish sun.

'Any news?' he asked, signalling to her to sit down. Ros Taylor shook her head.

'I'm afraid not. It looks as though this whole thing may have been a wild-goose chase after all.'

'Ah,' the Consul said, shaking his head. 'I am so sorry. Really. These cases are always so difficult.' Ros Taylor ran her fingers through her hair, and swallowed hard.

'My ex-husband may already have gone on somewhere else, taking the children with him. Back to France maybe. They were here, I'm sure of that.'

'I'm sorry,' the Consul said again. 'If there is anything I can—'

She shook her head.

'No. You've been very kind. I just came to let you know that I'm leaving this afternoon on the four o'clock flight. I have to be back at work on Monday. I just can't afford to take any more time off.'

'Of course. I quite understand. And we do have your address in London, don't we?'

She fished in her bag and pulled out an envelope which she handed to him.

'It's all in there. I've put photographs of both the children in as well. Someone might recognize them.'

'Good. I'll keep spreading the news around, discreetly, of course, and if we hear anything—'

'Anything at all . . . just phone me and I'll come straight back.' She shook her head. 'You know, I just can't believe I'm going home without them. I was so sure—' The Consul said nothing, although he nodded sympathetically. With an effort Ros Taylor stood up. 'Well, I mustn't take up any more of your time. I expect you're busy.'

They walked towards the door.

'Do you have kids?' she asked, turning to him.

'Grown-up ones,' the Consul smiled. 'And two grandchildren.'

'You're lucky then,' she said. 'It's a terrible thing to lose your children. Like losing a limb.' She frowned.

The Consul was afraid she was going to cry. He cleared his throat.

'Look,' he said, 'if there's anything further I can do, please don't hesitate to get in touch again. And, of course, if we hear anything—this is a small community, you know. It's always possible. You mustn't give up hope.'

'Thanks,' Ros Taylor said again. His hand was on the door handle and she could see that her time was up. Suddenly the bleakness of the return journey to the empty flat overwhelmed her, and shaking her head she left the room in a blur of tears.

Out in the hall the secretary was already opening the door to another visitor, but Ros Taylor was unaware of the figure standing on the steps. Anxious only to get out into the street, she rushed towards the door and the next moment she had collided violently with the large woman

103

standing there, almost sending her flying, and dislodging the bag that she was carrying so that it flew down the steps and landed on the path.

All at once she was apologizing.

'How clumsy of me. Please . . . let me help you. I am so sorry—'

'That's all right, ma'am,' the woman answered, as they bent down together to pick up the contents of the bag that were scattered across the path.

'Here,' Ros Taylor said, handing her a sheaf of papers.

And then she saw it, pinned to the outside of a large white envelope.

For a moment everything swam in front of her eyes and she thought she might faint.

'Sean,' she gasped. 'Sean . . . and Josie.' She looked up into the elderly, seamed face. 'These are my kids—'

'Your kids?'

'This piece from the paper . . . the photo . . . they're my kids. I've been out here searching for them for weeks . . . but how—'

'Well, honey, I can tell you where they are,' said the woman, putting her hand on Ros Taylor's arm to steady her. 'Because I saw them this morning.'

'You've seen them today?'

'Just before I drove down here,' the elderly American woman nodded. 'Fact is, it's your kids I've come to see the British Consul about. So why don't you come right back inside with me, and we can see him together. Then maybe we can get this whole mess sorted out.'


All day on Friday Sean waited for something to happen. As the day wore on, the air grew still and heavy, and it seemed to him that a feeling of doom hung over the farmhouse. Time was running out.

There's only today and tomorrow, he thought. By Sunday it will probably be too late.

In the morning he had been full of hope. Up on the mountain, he'd watched as Mrs Kauffman came down the steps from her apartment and climbed into her car. She'd never been out so early before and his spirits soared as he saw the small green car moving towards the road. He shaded his eyes, watching it vanish amongst the houses in the village and then re-emerge on the other side and begin its journey down the mountain to the coast. She had gone to fetch help. He was certain of it, and half expected to see policemen arriving at the *finca*.

But when Mrs Kauffman came back that afternoon she was alone. She climbed the steps to her apartment and went inside, closing the door behind her. Later, as they walked back down the hill and into the yard there was no sign of her and the shutters on the first floor were closed.

Soon afterwards his father and Isabella came back. Sean heard them talking before they got out of the car.

'I'll speak to the kids tonight,' his dad said. 'You can talk to Maria and Alonso.'

'*Si*,' Isabella said nodding.

'Tell them Sunday afternoon . . . explain . . . '

His dad was winding up the window as he spoke and Sean missed the rest, but he had guessed already. They really were going to America, and if Mrs Kauffman didn't do something quickly it would be too late. She had seemed like someone he could trust, Sean thought. But perhaps he'd been wrong. Perhaps she hadn't even read the piece in the newspaper.

'South America first,' his dad said when they were all inside. 'From there we'll work our way up to Florida.' He lifted Josie on to his knee. 'That's where Disneyland is—in Florida.' Josie was looking thoughtful. 'There's something else, too. Something I want to tell you both—' He looked across at Sean and then held out his hand to Isabella. 'When we get to South America,

105

Isabella and I are going to get married. Then we'll be a proper family, won't we?'

That means she's going to be my stepmother, Sean thought emptily, his eyes meeting Isabella's. She smiled at him, and for an instant Sean saw the look of triumph in her eyes.

Josie was kicking the table leg. 'I thought you were married to Mum,' she said.

'Not any more, sweetheart,' their dad said, kissing the top of her head. 'We're divorced now. That means I can marry Isabella.'

'Oh,' said Josie, her voice flat. She slid off his knee. 'I want to go and see the kittens now.'

'Don't you want to know some more about America?' Josie shook her head.

'No. I want to see the kittens.' And the next moment she was through the door and running across the farmyard with Isabella behind her.

'When are we going?' Sean asked, his voice hollow. He had to know how much longer they had.

'Sunday afternoon,' his dad said. 'Quarter past five. I'm going to pick up our tickets and travel documents in the morning. It'll be great, Sean,' he went on. 'A fresh start for all of us. You're going to love it, I promise you.'

But Sean had heard his dad's promises before.

'I'm going to clear up,' he said, turning on his heel.

Mrs Kauffman was packing up to leave, too. Sean could hear the sound of footsteps above, and things being put down on the floor. She was leaving, and she wasn't going to do anything to help after all. In the bedroom, he emptied the contents of his school bag on to the bed and began sorting everything out. After a while Josie came in. She closed the door softly behind her and sat beside him on the bed. Looking at her, Sean noticed for the first time how much thinner she'd grown. She seemed older too, her baby look quite gone.

'I don't want to go to America,' she said after a

moment, her voice low. 'Do you?' Sean shook his head. 'And I don't want Dad to marry Isabella,' she said.

'Nor do I,' Sean said. 'But we can't do anything about it.'

Josie was silent for a moment, looking at him.

'I want to see Mum,' she said at last. 'I want to go home again. Only Dad won't let us, will he? It's not fair.' Then glancing towards the door, she leaned across to him and whispered in his ear. 'Why don't we run away . . . both of us?'

Startled, Sean looked at her. He opened his mouth, and then closed it again, frowning, and wondering whether to tell her about Mrs Kauffman.

'Why don't we?' Josie said, still looking at him.

'I have been trying to think of a way,' Sean said slowly. 'I've been trying for a long time.'

'I know.' Josie nodded. 'Perhaps she'd help us,' she said after a moment, pointing towards the ceiling.

'Mrs Kauffman, you mean?' Sean asked, frowning. She nodded.

'She's nice. She stopped me falling.' Sean stared at her.

'You were awake—' Josie gave a little wriggle.

'Sort of,' she said. 'Don't you think she'd help us?'

Still Sean didn't dare tell her. Not everything. Not yet.

'I'll think about it,' he said. 'If I could work out a plan tonight, then tomorrow—'

'Yes,' Josie nodded. 'We can run away tomorrow, can't we?' She leant towards him again. 'Only it's got to be a secret, hasn't it?'

'Yes,' Sean said. 'Whatever happens you mustn't tell Dad—'

'Or Isabella.'

'Were you really awake?' Sean asked, looking at her thoughtfully.

'If I was, then it was only a little bit,' Josie said.

Suddenly he grinned. Josie wanted to go back home as

much as he did. That much was obvious. So why not tell her about Mrs Kauffman now? Not that it was going to be any good. But just in case. He stood up and went over to the door. His dad and Isabella were in the living room, talking. Then he turned back to Josie.

'Listen,' he said softly, 'I do have a sort of plan as it happens . . . ' And he began to explain.

The next day, Saturday, would be their last full day at the *finca*. On Sunday they were going to America.

By the next morning, things were already changing. For one thing, the Goat Man didn't come to take them to the mountains. He had been out in the yard at first light, helping Maria and Alonso to load the truck for market with the produce they were taking to sell. Then he had waved them goodbye.

'Isn't the Goat Man going to the market?' Josie asked.

'My uncle the Goat Man doesn't like to go to town,' Isabella said. 'Too many people . . . he likes to stay here in the quiet. Also it is a long day. My aunt and uncle will not be back till dark.'

After breakfast their father went off to pick up the airline tickets.

'Back by lunch time,' he told Isabella.

At the door he turned and looked back, as though he half expected one of them to come after him. Not so long ago Josie would have been begging to go. But she just sat at the table, turning the pages of her Peter and Jane reading book.

'Well, be good,' he said.

'We will.' Josie nodded, not looking up.

'See you when I get back.'

'OK,' Sean said. There was a tight knot in his stomach. If Mrs Kauffman was going to do anything it would have to be this morning after their dad had driven off. Sean wished he would just go. But still he hesitated. He frowned, patting his shirt pocket.

'Dark glasses,' he said.

'There,' said Isabella. 'On the dresser.' She threw the

rope of hair over her shoulder. 'You forget your head next, Harvey.'

He pulled a face and winked at Sean. Then, dropping a kiss on the top of Josie's head he went out, and a moment later they heard the car drive off.

Isabella was sorting out piles of T-shirts and shorts on the ironing board. She had bolted the front door, Sean noticed. That meant there was no chance of them going outside. He looked across at Josie, who calmly turned another page.

' "Peter and Jane go for a . . . " What's that word?' she asked, pushing the book over to Sean.

'Picnic,' he said. ' "Peter and Jane go for a picnic . . . " '

Isabella had plugged in the iron and was starting on the shirts. Sean took some paper out of his school bag and drew out a game of boxes.

He'd finished the first two lines when they heard footsteps outside. Then there was a knock at the door.

Isabella stood still, listening, the iron held in mid-air. Sean looked up. His heart was beating hard against his ribs.

'Who's that?' Josie asked in a loud voice. Isabella frowned and shook her head, holding a finger to her lips. A moment later the knocking came again.

'Aren't you going to answer it?' Sean asked.

'No . . . ' She shook her head. 'No . . . '

He went across to the window and Josie ran after him.

'It's the American lady from upstairs,' he said.

'Coo-ee,' came a voice from outside. 'Anyone home?'

Then, before Isabella could stop her, Josie was tapping on the window and waving.

'You'd better answer it,' Sean said, looking at Isabella. 'It'll seem pretty funny if you don't. She knows we're here.'

Isabella slammed the iron down. Sean grinned.

'You two are to stay in here,' she hissed, going to the door.

Josie was excited now. She clutched at Sean's arm.

'This is the plan, isn't it?' she whispered as Isabella drew back the bolt and opened the door just far enough to look out.

'I think so,' Sean nodded. 'Listen . . . '

They could hear Mrs Kauffman's voice now.

'Good morning,' she was saying. 'Excuse me troubling you, but you know I'm leaving today, around noon, and I wondered whether you could tell me what to do with the key? I've been across to the house, but there doesn't seem to be anyone there—'

'They have gone to the market,' Isabella said.

'Ah, I see. And the keys?'

'You can leave them in the apartment,' Isabella said. 'I will tell my aunt.' She was starting to close the door. Sean could see the fingers of her hand spread out, pushing it. Only Mrs Kauffman hadn't finished.

'Thank you, dear,' she said. 'If you're sure that will be all right. Oh, and there is just one other thing. There's some food left in the fridge. I wondered whether your family might like to use it up—I do so hate waste. So please—'

'*Si* . . . ?'

'Please ask your aunt to take it.'

'Thank you, *señora*.' Isabella started to close the door again, but this time Josie was too fast for her. Skipping across the room she wriggled round Isabella and stood, looking up at Mrs Kauffman.

'Why, hello, dear,' Mrs Kauffman said before Isabella could push Josie back inside. 'How are you today?'

'Very well, thank you,' Josie said.

'And what's your name?'

'Josie.' She smiled her best smile. Sean edged over to the door and stood behind her.

'Josie . . . my, what a pretty name. They've been so good,' Mrs Kauffman went on, turning back to Isabella. 'I never knew such well behaved children . . . there's a boy, too, isn't there? Yes, I thought so. Ah, there you are, dear. I was just saying how good and quiet you've

110

been since I arrived. Do you know I've hardly heard you and your sister at all.' She turned to Isabella again. 'Now, you wouldn't mind if I took a photograph of them before I go, would you?' Isabella was blocking the doorway with her body, one hand on Josie's shoulder. 'As a souvenir, you know.'

'You can take my picture if you like,' Josie said.

'Well, fine, honey.' Mrs Kauffman smiled.

'No,' Isabella said. 'No, that is not possible . . . '

Mrs Kauffman spoke quickly, still smiling at Isabella. 'Come now! It'll only take a moment. And you're welcome to be in it as well, if you like.' Isabella shook her head. 'OK—camera shy, eh?' She nodded. 'So—just the kids then . . . what about it, you two?'

Sean didn't hesitate any longer. He pushed past Isabella and grabbed Josie's hand.

'We'd both like to be in the picture,' he said.

'Well now, isn't that polite.' Mrs Kauffman nodded approvingly. 'How about the top of the steps . . . I think that would be good, don't you?'

Isabella wiped her hands down her jeans and glanced quickly round the farmyard. But there was no one there to help, and already Sean and Josie were following Mrs Kauffman up the steps. She ran after them.

'Their papa will be angry—' she began.

'Nonsense, dear,' Mrs Kauffman cut in. 'This won't take a moment. Besides, he's not here, is he? So he'll never know. And when we've taken the picture I have some ice cream waiting . . . Strawberry ice cream . . . '

And so, still talking, she led them up the steps. When they reached the top, Mrs Kauffman put a strong hand on their shoulders, and guided them forward into the darkness of the shuttered room. Sean was aware of a pile of luggage and the smell of oil paint, and of Mrs Kauffman suddenly talking what sounded like gibberish.

'Step up, step up and be saved,' she was chanting in her deep American voice. 'Straight ahead for salvation, my dears. Just a few more steps and we'll be there.'

Somewhere behind them Isabella had started to shout. And then another door was opened and they found themselves stumbling forward into a sudden flood of light.

'See and behold!' Mrs Kauffman said.

And Sean saw . . . his mum, standing there, just a few steps away from them holding out her arms, and for one perfect moment it was just the way he'd imagined it would be.

Then Isabella was in the room with them, shouting in Spanish, and things began to happen very quickly, just like they had at the beginning, on the day Sean had come out of school and heard the car horn hooting.

'I don't think you'll be wanted in here, dear,' Mrs Kauffman said, trying to catch hold of Isabella as she darted towards Josie.

And then Sean's mum thrust them both behind her and faced Isabella across the table.

'You just stop right where you are,' she said in a voice that would have cut rocks. 'These are *my* kids and they're coming with me. And whoever you are, I can tell you, you're not going to stop me now.'

All at once a man was opening the back door, and they were running down the back steps and towards a car that waited further up the track.

'Run, both of you, run . . . ' Ros Taylor shouted.

But Isabella was close behind them and running faster than they were. Already she was reaching out her arm towards Josie. She might have caught her, too, only from nowhere it seemed a tall figure had appeared in their path and, holding out an arm, he caught Isabella, stopping her in her tracks and holding on tight as she struggled and shrieked.

From behind them, Sean heard Mrs Kauffman give a cheer, and then they had reached the car.

'Get in the back,' the man told them. 'Quick!'

The car door was slammed shut and a moment later they were moving forward. Looking out of the back window, Sean could see Isabella, running, running, running along the track after them, with her plait undone and her hair blowing wild across her face, while behind her the Goat Man raised his arm in a last salute.

'Slow down,' Sean cried. 'Please. I want to wind down the window and wave goodbye.'

'Better not,' said the man at the wheel, catching their mum's eye in the mirror and shaking his head.

Through the back window Sean could see the Goat Man, still waving.

'Who was that?' Ros Taylor asked.

'The Goat Man,' Josie told her. 'He looked after us. But he couldn't speak.'

'Couldn't speak?'

'Dumb,' said Sean. He saw his mum give a shudder. 'It's all right,' he said. 'Really. He was our friend. Only I didn't really know until now.'

Josie nodded. 'He stopped Isabella catching me,' she said.

'I think he had one of the saddest faces I have ever seen,' Ros Taylor said. And then, looking from one to the other of them, and smiling through tears. 'Look at you! Just look at you both. You're so brown. And thin . . . and your hair . . . just look at your hair—'

'That's because you didn't come and fetch us,' Josie said, suddenly cross. 'Why didn't you come? We missed you and missed you, didn't we, Sean? And you still didn't come.'

'Well, I'm here now,' Ros Taylor said, hugging them both closer as the car roared on down the mountain road.

'Where are we going?' Sean asked after a while. 'I mean—what will happen next?'

'Straight to the airport,' his mum said. 'The Consul has arranged everything . . . tickets, passports for you two, the lot. We're going home.'

'Home?' said Josie, with a kind of wonder in her voice.

Ros Taylor nodded. 'We'll be back by tea time.'

'Promise?' said Sean.

'Promise,' she said.

# 14

'But what was it like?' Tinker would ask over and over
again. 'I mean—what was it *really* like?'

Pushing his glasses up his nose, he'd stare at Sean.

'I told you,' Sean would mutter. 'Boring.'

'Not all the time,' Tinker would frown.

'Mostly,' Sean said, his gaze wandering restlessly
round the room.

Tinker would sigh. Things weren't a bit the way he'd
expected. He'd thought that everything would just go
back to how it had been before. But Sean was different
since he'd come home. He didn't seem to want to talk
about Spain. He didn't even seem specially interested in
how Tinker had seen him and Josie on video at Mr and
Mrs Clatworthy's house. And instead of wanting to get
on with things, he seemed mostly to stare into space.

'Give him time,' Ros Taylor had said. 'It hasn't been
easy for him or Josie. A lot has happened since they
went away.'

Tinker couldn't quite understand that. If so much had
happened then why did Sean keep saying it had been
boring? And there was another thing. He seemed to
want to spend more time with Josie than he ever had
before. Tinker felt hard done by.

If it wasn't for me, he thought, Sean would be in
South America by this time. And so would Josie.

Sean knew that really. When his mum had first told
him the story of how Tinker had seen him and Josie on
someone's home video it had seemed like a kind of
miracle.

'A bit like winning the lottery, only better,' Ros Taylor had laughed, hugging them both all over again.

It was just that Tinker went on and on about it, and Sean didn't really want to think about that evening in the square. There were lots of things he didn't want to think about. The trouble was, he couldn't stop himself. Josie was remembering too, but in a different way. Sometimes Sean thought that Josie was the only person who understood how he felt.

Home seemed to have changed since they went away. After the huge silence of the mountains, London was noisier than he remembered, and there didn't seem to be room to move around any more. Sometimes, lying on his bed and staring out of the window at the line of roofs behind their building, it seemed to Sean that the bedroom walls were moving in towards him. When that happened he wanted to jump up and shout and breathe in great gusts of fresh air. Even in class he found it hard to sit still. He was always looking for an excuse to get up and walk about. It was hard to concentrate. Things kept running through his mind and he couldn't stop them. Right in the middle of some lesson a thought would come walloping into his head, about the *finca*, or the mountain, or Isabella, and off he'd go, like a jerky old film, playing the same bit over and over again. He thought quite a bit about the Goat Man too, remembering the day down by the river when he'd made the boats for them out of walnut shells, or seeing the tall figure striding ahead of them up the mountain, with all the leaping goats around him. And then he would remember how the Goat Man had put out his arm and stopped Isabella, holding her even though she struggled and shouted while they ran to the car. I believe he'd guessed from the beginning, Sean thought. But of course he'd never know for sure.

The worst part was remembering what had happened at the airport. It would have been all right if his dad hadn't followed them. But suddenly there he was, coming towards them through the crowd, pushing people out of the way and shouting that he wanted his kids. They were just about to go through Passport Control when it happened.

'Oh, my God,' their mum had said. 'Quick . . . come on, both of you. Hurry. We've got to get to the other side . . . then he won't be able to reach us. Don't look round. Don't . . . '

And all the time they were moving up the queue, until suddenly their dad spotted them just as they arrived in front of the man who was checking the passports, and he came running towards them, his face looking all strange and unreal, as if he was somebody else. That was what Sean couldn't forget. Then the Consul who had come with them to the airport came between them and told the man in Spanish to check the passports quickly and push them through, so that suddenly they were on the other side of the glass partition where their dad couldn't reach them, and he was shouting and shouting and the tears were running down his face.

'Oh, my God. Oh, my God,' Sean's mum had said, over and over again, and more than anything at that moment Sean had wanted to go back and explain and say goodbye properly, because he could see how much his dad really loved them and how unhappy it would make him going to South America without them. But it was too late.

He does love us, Sean thought. He really, really does.

And in spite of everything that had happened, that was the hardest thing of all, because Sean knew that his dad wouldn't be able to come back home for a long time, not with him having kidnapped them. And so there was no telling when he and Josie would see him again.

About a month after they arrived back Mrs Kauffman came to visit them one Saturday afternoon, on her way home to America. She had a large bag with her made out of some kind of carpet, and she sat at their kitchen table drinking tea and eating chocolate biscuits just as though they were all old friends. After her second cup of tea and her third chocolate biscuit, Mrs Kauffman opened her carpet bag and took out presents for Sean and Josie. Josie's was a Spanish dress, and when their mum had gone to help her try it on, Mrs Kauffman gave Sean his present. It was large and flat and not very well wrapped up, and when he opened it he saw that it was one of her paintings of the mountain behind the *finca*.

Sean stared at the picture, trying not to look disappointed, but not knowing what to say. He couldn't understand why Mrs Kauffman had given it to him. But it seemed that Mrs Kauffman did, because when Sean muttered some kind of thank you, she waved her hand and said, 'That mountain is part of you now and you'll never be able to forget it. So you'd better live with it.'

After Mrs Kauffman had gone, his mum had fixed a string to the back of the picture so that he could hang it on his wall. After a while Sean found that he quite liked looking at it when he was lying in bed. He would remember the ring of mountains and the bleating of the goats, and the cries of the birds as they circled high above. And he would remember the Goat Man, too. In a funny kind of way it did make him feel better.

At Easter their mum took them to the Yorkshire Dales for a week. There were mountains there, too, great lines of bare, rolling hills, and as they went about each day, walking in the clean, cold wind, Sean forgot Spain and began to feel much better.

The day after they arrived home, he said he was going to phone Tinker. His mum nodded and looked pleased.

'Hi,' Sean said when he got through.

'Hi,' said Tinker.

'Want to come round and finish that model we were making?' Sean asked. And Tinker, at the other end of the line, pushed his glasses up his nose and grinned.

'Yeah,' he said, trying not to sound too keen. 'OK then. If you like.'

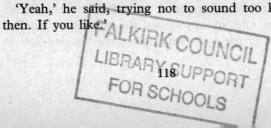